Edgar Fawcett, Robert Green Ingersoll

Agnosticism and other essays

Edgar Fawcett, Robert Green Ingersoll

Agnosticism and other essays

ISBN/EAN: 9783743463523

Manufactured in Europe, USA, Canada, Australia, Japa

Cover: Foto ©Andreas Hilbeck / pixelio.de

Manufactured and distributed by brebook publishing software (www.brebook.com)

Edgar Fawcett, Robert Green Ingersoll

Agnosticism and other essays

OTHER ESSAYS

BY

EDGAR FAWCETT

WITH A PROLOGUE BY

ROBERT G. INGERSOLL

New York, Chicago, and San Francisco

BELFORD, CLARKE AND COMPANY

PUBLISHERS

London : II. J. Drane, Lovell's Court, Paternoster Row

... is a form of faith which prevents manly inquiry "

Dinsmore

Unquestioned faith amounts to thought to a reverence only worthy of a savage

" ' *Heaven help us !* ' *said the old religion ; the new one, from its very lack of that faith, will teach us all the more to help one another.*"

—GEORGE ELIOT'S LETTERS.

ROBERT G. INGERSOLL'S PRO-LOGUE.

I.

EDGAR FAWCETT.

EDGAR FAWCETT—a great poet, a meta-physician and logician—has been for years engaged in exploring that strange world wherein are supposed to be the springs of human action. He has sought for some-thing back of motives, reasons, fancies, pas-sions, prejudices, and the countless tides and tendencies that constitute the life of man.

He has found some of the limitations of mind, and knows that beginning at that luminous centre called consciousness, a few short steps bring us to the prison wall where vision fails and all light dies. Be-yond this wall the eternal darkness broods. This gloom is "the other world" of the

supernaturalist. With him, real vision begins where the sight fails. He reverses
the order of nature. Facts become illusions, and illusions the only realities. He
believes that the cause of the image, the
reality, is behind the mirror.

A few centuries ago the priests said to
their followers : The other world is above
you ; it is just beyond where you see. Afterwards the astronomer with his telescope
looked, and asked the priests : Where is
the world of which you speak? And the
priests replied : It has receded—it is just
beyond where you see.

As long as there is "a beyond" there is
room for the priests' world. Theology is
the geography of this beyond.

Between the Christian and the Agnostic
there is the difference of assertion and
question—between "There is a God" and
"Is there a God?" The Agnostic has the
arrogance to admit his ignorance, while
the Christian from the depths of humility
impudently insists that he knows.

Mr. Fawcett has shown that at the root
of religion lies the coiled serpent of fear,
and that ceremony, prayer, and worship
are ways and means to gain the assistance
or soften the heart of a supposed deity.

He also shows that as man advances in knowledge he loses confidence in the watchfulness of Providence and in the effi-cacy of prayer.

II.

SCIENCE.

THE savage is certain of those things that cannot be known. He is acquainted with origin and destiny, and knows every-thing except' that which is useful. The civilized man, having outgrown the igno-rance, the arrogance, and the provincialism of savagery, abandons the vain search for final causes, for the nature and origin of things.

In nearly every department of science man is allowed to investigate, and the dis-covery of a new fact is welcomed, unless it threatens some creed.

Of course there can be no advance in a religion established by infinite wisdom. The only progress possible is in the com-prehension of this religion.

For many generations what is known under a vast number of disguises and be-hind many masks as the Christian relig-ion has been propagated and preserved by

the sword and bayonet—that is to say, by
force. The credulity of man has been
bribed and his reason punished. Those
who believed without the slightest question, and whose faith held evidence in
contempt, were saints ; those who inves-
tigated were dangerous, and those who
denied were destroyed.

Every attack upon this religion has been
made in the shadow of human and divine
hatred—in defiance of earth and heaven.
At one time Christendom was beneath the
ignorant feet of one man, and those who
denied his infallibility were heretics and
atheists.   At last a protest was uttered.
The right of conscience was proclaimed, to
the extent of making a choice between the
infallible man and the infallible book.
Those who rejected the man and accepted
the book became in their turn as merciless, as tyrannical and heartless, as the followers of the infallible man. The Protestants insisted that an infinitely wise and
good God would not allow criminals and
wretches to act as his infallible agents.

Afterwards a few protested against the
infallibility of the book, using the same
arguments against the book that had for-
merly been used against the pope. They

said that an infinitely wise and good God could not be the author of a cruel and ignorant book. But those who protested against the book fell into substantially the same error that had been fallen into by those who had protested against the man. While they denounced the book, and insisted that an infinitely wise and good being could not have been its author, they took the ground that an infinitely wise and good being was the creator and governor of the world. -

Then was used against them the same argument that had been used by the Protestants against the pope and by the Deists against the Protestants. Attention was called to the fact that Nature is as cruel as any pope or any book—that it is just as easy to account for the destruction of the Canaanites consistently with the goodness of Jehovah as to account for pestilence, earthquake, and flood consistently with the goodness of the God of Nature.

The Protestant and Deist both used arguments against the Catholic that could in turn be used with equal force against themselves. So that there is no question among intelligent people as to the infallibility of the pope, as to the inspiration of the book, or as to the existence of the Christian's God—for the conclusion has been reached that the human mind is incapable of deciding as to the origin and destiny of the universe.

For many generations the mind of man has been travelling in a circle. It accepted without question the dogma of a First Cause—of the existence of a Creator—of an Infinite Mind back of matter, and sought in many ways to define its ignorance in this behalf. The most sincere worshippers have declared that this Being is incomprehensible,—that he is "without body, parts, or passions"—that he is infinitely beyond their grasp,—and at the same time have insisted that it was necessary for man not only to believe in the existence of this Being, but to love him with all his heart.

Christianity having always been in partnership with the State,—having controlled kings and nobles, judges and legislators— having been in partnership with armies and with every form of organized destruction,—it was dangerous to discuss the foundation of its authority. To speak lightly of any dogma was a crime punishable by death. Every absurdity has been bastioned and barricaded by the power of the State. It has been protected by fist, by club, by sword and cannon. For many years Christianity succeeded in substantially closing the mouths of its enemies, and lived and flourished only where investigation and discussion were prevented by hypocrisy and bigotry. The Church still talks about "evidence," about "reason," about "freedom of conscience" and the "liberty of speech," and yet denounces those who ask for evidence, who appeal to reason, and who honestly express their thoughts.

To-day we know that the miracles of Christianity are as puerile and false as those ascribed to the medicine-men of Central Africa or the Fiji Islanders, and that the "sacred scriptures" have the same claim to inspiration that the Koran has or the Book of Mormon—no less, no more. These questions have been settled and laid aside by free and intelligent people. They have ceased to excite interest; and the man who now really believes in the truth of the Old Testament is regarded with a smile—looked upon as an aged child—still satisfied with the lullabys and toys of the cradle.

III.

MORALITY.

It is contended that without religion—that is to say, without Christianity—all ideas of morality must of necessity perish, and that spirituality and reverence will be lost.

What is morality?

Is it to obey without question, or is it to act in accordance with perceived obligation? Is it something with which intelligence has nothing to do? Must the ignorant child carry out the command of the wise father—the rude peasant rush to death at the request of the prince?

Is it impossible for morality to exist where the brain and heart are in partnership? Is there no foundation for morality except punishment threatened or reward promised by a superior to an inferior? If this be true, how can the superior be virtuous? Cannot the reward and the threat be in the nature of things? Can they not rest in consequences perceived by the intellect? How can the existence or non-existence of a deity change my obligation to keep my hands out of the fire?

The results of all actions are equally certain, but not equally known, not equally perceived. If all men knew with perfect certainty that to steal from another was to rob themselves, larceny would cease. It cannot be said too often that actions are good or bad in the light of consequences, and that a clear perception of consequences would control actions. That which increases the sum of human happiness is moral ; that which diminishes the sum of human happiness is immoral. Blind, unreasoning obedience is the enemy of morality. Slavery is not the friend of virtue. Actions are neither right nor wrong by virtue of what men or gods can say ; the right or wrong lives in results— in the nature of things, growing out of relations violated or caused.

Accountability lives in the nature of consequences—in their absolute certainty—in the fact that they cannot be placated, avoided, or bribed.

The relations of human life are too complicated to be accurately and clearly understood, and, as a consequence, rules of action vary from age to age. The ideas of right and wrong change with the experience of the race, and this change is wrought by the gradual ascertaining of consequences—of results. For this reason the religion of one age fails to meet the standard of another, precisely as the laws that satisfied our ancestors are repealed by us ; so that, in spite of all efforts, religion itself is subject to gradual and perpetual change.

The miraculous is no longer the basis of morals. Man is a sentient being—he suffers and enjoys. In order to be happy he must preserve the conditions of well-being —must live in accordance with certain facts by which he is surrounded. If he violates these conditions the result is unhappiness, failure, disease, misery.

Man must have food, roof, raiment, fireside, friends—that is to say, prosperity; and this he must earn—this he must deserve. He is no longer satisfied with being a slave, even of the Infinite. He wishes to perceive for himself, to understand, to investigate, to experiment ; and he has at last the courage to bear the consequences that he brings upon himself. He has also found that those who are the most religious are not always the kindest, and that those who have been and are the worshippers of God enslave their fellow-men. He has found that there is no necessary connection between religion and morality.

Morality needs no supernatural assistance —needs neither miracle nor pretence. It has nothing to do with awe, reverence, credulity, or blind, unreasoning faith. Morality is the highway perceived by the soul, the direct road, leading to success, honor, and happiness.

The best thing to do under the circumstances is moral.

The highest possible standard is human. We put ourselves in the places of others. We are made happy by the kindness of others, and we feel that a fair exchange of good actions is the wisest and best commerce. We know that others can make us miserable by acts of hatred and injustice, and we shrink from inflicting the pain upon others that we have felt ourselves : this is the foundation of conscience.

If man could not suffer, the words right and wrong could never have been spoken.

The agnostic, the infidel, clearly perceives the true basis of morals, and, so perceiving, he knows that the religious man, the superstitious man, caring more for God than for his fellows, will sacrifice his fellows, either at the supposed command of

his God, or to win his approbation. He
also knows that the religionist has no basis
for morals except these supposed com-
mands. The basis of morality with him
lies not in the nature of things, but in the
caprice of some deity. He seems to think
that, had it not been for the Ten Command-
ments, larceny and murder might have
been virtues.

IV.

SPIRITUALITY.

WHAT is it to be spiritual?

Is this fine quality of the mind destroyed
by the development of the brain? As the
domain wrested by science from ignorance
increases—as island after island and continent after continent are discovered—as
star after star and constellation after constellation in the intellectual world burst
upon the midnight of ignorance, does the
spirituality of the mind grow less and
less? Like morality, is it only found in the
company of ignorance and superstition? Is
the spiritual man honest, kind, candid?—or
dishonest, cruel, and hypocritical? Does
he say what he thinks? Is he guided by
reason? Is he the friend of the right?—

the champion of the truth? Must this
splendid quality called spirituality be re-
tained through the loss of candor? Can
we not truthfully say that absolute candor
is the beginning of wisdom?

To recognize the finer harmonies of conduct—to live to the ideal—to separate the
incidental, the evanescent, from the perpetual—to be enchanted with the perfect
melody of truth—open to the influences of
the artistic, the beautiful, the heroic—to
shed kindness as the sun sheds light—to
recognize the good in others, and to include
the world in the idea of self—this is to be
spiritual.

There is nothing spiritual in the worship
of the unknown and unknowable, in the
self-denial of a slave at the command of a
master whom he fears. Fastings, prayings,
mutilations, kneelings, and mortifications
are either the results of, or result in, insanity. This is the spirituality of Bedlam,
and is of no kindred with the soul that
finds its greatest joy in the discharge of
obligation perceived.

V.

REVERENCE.

WHAT is reverence?

It is the feeling produced when we stand in the presence of our ideal, or of that which most nearly approaches it—that which is produced by what we consider the highest degree of excellence.

The highest is reverenced, praised, and admired without qualification. Each man reverences according to his nature, his experience, his intellectual development. He may reverence Nero or Marcus Aurelius, Jehovah or Buddha, the author of Leviticus or Shakespeare. Thousands of men reverence John Calvin, Torquemada, and the Puritan fathers; and some have greater respect for Jonathan Edwards than for Captain Kidd.

A vast number of people have great reverence for anything that is covered by mould, or moss, or mildew. They bow low before rot and rust, and adore the worthless things that have been saved by the negligence of oblivion. They are enchanted with the dull and fading daubs of the old masters, and hold in contempt those miracles of art, the paintings of to-day. They worship the ancient, the shadowy, the mysterious, the wonderful. They doubt the value of anything that they understand.

The creed of Christendom is the enemy of morality. It teaches that the innocent can justly suffer for the guilty, that consequences can be avoided by repentance, and that in the world of mind the great fact known as cause and effect does not apply.

It is the enemy of spirituality, because it teaches that credulity is of more value than conduct, and because it pours contempt upon human love by raising far above it the adoration of a phantom.

It is the enemy of reverence. It makes ignorance the foundation of virtue. It belittles the useful, and cheapens the noblest of the virtues. It teaches man to live on mental alms, and glorifies the intellectual pauper. It holds candor in contempt, and is the malignant foe of mental manhood.

VI.

EXISTENCE OF GOD.

MR. FAWCETT has shown conclusively that it is no easier to establish the existence of an infinitely wise and good being by the

existence of what we call "good" than to
establish the existence of an infinitely bad
being by what we call "bad."

Nothing can be surer than that the history of this world furnishes no foundation
on which to base an inference that it has
been governed by infinite wisdom and
goodness. So terrible has been the condition of man that religionists in all ages have
endeavored to excuse God by accounting
for the evils of the world by the wickedness
of men. And the Fathers of the Christian
Church were forced to take the ground
that this world had been filled with briers
and thorns, with deadly serpents and with
poisonous weeds, with disease and crime
and earthquake and pestilence and storm,
by the curse of God.

The probability is that no God has
cursed, and that no God will bless, this
earth. Man suffers and enjoys according
to conditions. The sun shines without love,
and the lightning blasts without hate.
Man is the Providence of man.

Nature gives to our eyes all they can see,
to our ears all they can hear, and to the
mind what it can comprehend. The human
race reaps the fruit of every victory won on
the fields of intellectual or physical conflict.

We have no right to expect something for nothing. ⌈Man will reap no harvest the seeds of which he has not sown.⌋

The race must be guided by intelligence, must be free to investigate, and must have the courage and the candor not only to state what is known, but to cheerfully admit the limitations of the mind.

No intelligent, honest man can read what Mr. Fawcett has written and then say that he knows the origin and destiny of things— that he knows ·whether an Infinite Being exists or not, that he knows whether the soul of man is or is not immortal.

In the land of ———, the geography of which is not certainly known, there was for many years a great dispute among the inhabitants as to which road led to the City of Miragia, the capital of their country, and known to be the most delightful city on the earth. For fifty generations the discussion as to which road led to the city had been carried on with the greatest bitterness, until finally the people were divided into a great number of parties, each party claiming that the road leading to the city had been miraculously made known to the founder of that particular sect. The various parties spent most of their time putting up guide-boards on these roads and tearing down the guide-boards of others. Hundreds of thousands had been killed, prisons were filled, and the fields had been ravaged by the hosts of war.

One day, a wise man, a patriot, wishing to bring peace to his country, met the leaders of the various sects and asked them whether it was absolutely certain that the City of Miragia existed. He called their attention to the facts that no resident of that city had ever visited them and that none of their fellow-men who had started for the capital had ever returned, and modestly asked whether it would not be better to satisfy themselves beyond a doubt that there was such a city, adding that the location of the city would determine which of all the roads was the right one.

The leaders heard these words with amazement. They denounced the speaker as a wretch without morality, spirituality, or reverence, and thereupon he was torn in pieces.

ROBERT G. INGERSOLL.

PART II.

AGNOSTICISM.

RATIONALISM owes a debt of gratitude to *HW* him who coined the word "agnostic." Previously there had been only "infidel" and "atheist," and one or two other similar terms, all irate bayonets pointed at the very teeth of orthodoxy. They were words, too, that had attained a kind of rowdy, buccaneering prominence ; they appeared to prowl, like verbal guerillas, upon the outskirts of accepted vocabularies. Besides, they failed clearly to express, in many cases, the mental attitudes of those to whom they were applied. A good many sensible and moral people abode in the world who felt as averse to denying the existence of a deity as they did to affirming it. They resembled, to a certain degree, the chancellor in Tennyson's " Sleeping Beauty," who diplomatically

" Dallied with his golden chain and smiling put the
 question by."

Still, about the real agnostic spirit there is much more sincerity than diplomacy. It means, in its finest sense, a courageous envisaging of the awful problems of life and death, and an admission of their total insolubility. It might almost, in particular temperaments and personalities, be said to have become a sort of new religion by itself, simpler than that of Comte, with his complex and deliberated apings of Christian forms, and yet capable in some respects of being classed with Positivism. At the same time, a very large majority of agnostics are quite without the reverential sense. "I do not know" precludes in them all tendency to "divine" or to "feel." Nor should they be blamed for this indifference, reluctance, or whatever it may be called. Emotion and reason have an arctic and antarctic divergence.

The average type of agnostic has reached his present position through the help of reason, and therefore he cannot be expected to abandon the power which has made him what he is. That power would not desert him, indeed, even if he should try to exorcise it. He recognizes this truth and so patiently accepts the ally with which destiny has provided him. If he leans

toward absolute atheism—toward a denial
of any conscious and intelligent ruler
of the universe—he does so because vast
weight of evidence impels him. in that
direction, while a comparatively small influence lures him in another. Not long ago
an eminent thinker said to me, in a moment
of colloquial confidence : "Truly, the most
extraordinary idea which ever entered the
brain of man is that of a personal, over-
watching deity." Most modern agnostics
may be said to hold precisely this amazed
view of the case. And yet they will not
deny the deity either of ecclesiastic faith or
of operative imagination. No one has ever
seen the other side of the moon, and if you
were to tell an agnostic that you felt sure
this concealed lunar hemisphere was blazing
with active volcanoes he would not consider
himself authorized to deny your statement.
He might seriously doubt it, but he would
not deny it. His quarrel with the atheist
is not bitter, but it is appreciable. The
latter declares "There is no god," but the
former, firmly as he may believe so, scorns
assertion based upon partial proof. "Until
I have solved the secret of the universe,"
says the agnostic, "I shall forbear from
stating how, why or by whom it was

created." He realizes just how potent an Œdipus is requisite to make the Sphinx cast herself into the sea.

What, may be asked, are the causes which lead agnosticism to doubt that an almighty, tutelary and merciful power dwells behind the manifestations of nature? In the first place one might almost affirm that the good and evil which we see around us make any kind of conscious beneficent power beyond them a self-contradiction if not a nullity. For it is hard to conceive of a virtuous and omnipotent god permitting misery such as that with which our planet teems, and it is equally hard to conceive of a diabolic and omnipotent god not stamping out the happiness which also certainly abounds upon earth. John Stuart Mill has suggested the possibility of there being two gods forever at war with one another, from whose perpetual contest all admirable and deplorable things result; but this acute English thinker has touched upon the idea of such a celestial antagonism with a delicacy that might be defined as the irony of metaphysics, and no one more clearly apprehended than did he the complete idleness of mere *a priori* speculation. Again, agnosticism has to-day con-

vinced itself that all religions bear the sure
evidence of having originated solely in
man's intercourse with his fellow-men. At
the root of all worship lies one element—
that of fear, and the fear-begotten desire
to propitiate some hostile though viewless
agency. Christianity, and other creeds de-
pendent upon a so-called "revelation," have
never produced a single authentic proof of
their validity. Waiving members of the
Brahmin, the Buddhist, the Mohammedan,
the Parsee, and of other noteworthy faiths,
no Christian would at the present time accept for an instant as credible any fact so
faintly supported by historic *data* as that
of the alleged miraculous birth of Christ,
not to mention his having turned water
into wine, his having caused a dead man
to live again, or his having defied the laws
of gravitation by floating up into the sky
and so disappearing before the gaze of a
multitude. But the Christian insists upon
accepting as facts these follies redolent of
the grossest ignorance and superstition.
The Christian unhesitatingly asserts, too,
that morality is a product of direct revelation from some sort of anthropomorphic
spirit to mankind, instead of having been
gradually evolved through slow stages of

civilization, which began at a condition
lower than barbarism or cannibalism. The
Christian clings to this astonishing tenet
in the face of all that science has so ably
and amply taught him to the contrary.
And yet he by no means rejects the copious
and precious teachings of science. He respects them, indeed, with all the practical
ardor of an agnostic. If the wind blows
harsh from the east he does not content
himself with praying to his god that it
may fail to inflict pneumonia upon his favorite child. He bids that child button
stout wraps about the person and avoid
breathing too deeply the icy air. No
amount of trust in "providence" would
induce him to let a bushel of rotting vege-
tables pollute his cellar for a single day.
When he or any one dear to him is ill, he
seeks physician and not parson. Even if
he be a Roman Catholic, he gives the calo-
mel or the quinine, the nux vomica or the
bismuth, full curative scope, before he wel-
comes the hollow mummery of extreme unc-
tion. In all his goings and comings, among
all the details of his daily routine, the
Christian is quite as much a servant and
devotee of scientific discovery and testi-
mony as the most pronounced agnostic

who ever smiled at the absurdities of an
Adam, an Eve and an Eden. He will tell
you one minute that a benign tenderness and
compassion are forever invisibly befriending
him, and he will refer, the next, to having
taken passage for Europe on a particular
line of steamers because that is notorious-
ly the safest. If his house be insufficiently
guarded against lightning and yet be
struck some day without injury resulting
to any of its occupants, he will fall on his
knees, most probably, in heartfelt thanks-
giving to a kindly and protective personality whose august will forges the thunder-
bolt and determines its flight. But on the
following day he will be sure, if he can afford it, to have the whole house well-
equipped with lightning-rods.

From proofs like these the agnostic finds
himself arguing that the Christian does not
believe half so implicitly as he is under the
impression that he believes. For, if his belief were absolute, he would ignore his natural environment a great deal more than he
already does, in a fixed certainty that what
was to be would be, and that from first to
last his mortal career was under a clement
and sympathizing guardianship. Or, if it
were really credited by the Christian that

human ills befall the faithful as blessings in disguise, then he would nerve himself to receive such apparent disasters with ten times that stoicism which we now see him exhibit.

That any other than a god of exquisite cruelty should inflict these disasters upon mankind while the centuries continue to roll along, puzzles the agnostic in marked degree. Nothing is more common than to hear, from enthusiastic Christians, words that express passionate encomium of the grandeur and splendor of creation. "How could all this beauty and magnificence ex-ist," they cry, "unless a god of surpassing worth and wisdom produced them?" But they forget that for every agreeable or alluring feature there is one correspondingly odious and repellent. If the rose blooms, the poisonous plant thrives as well. If the sky bends blue and lucid above us, the tempest, with shafts of death and hurricanes of ruin, also has its reign there. If health glows in certain faces, disease ravages others. If sanity is the blessed endowment of many minds, madness is to many a curse and bane. If sexual love finds often its rightful and genial gratification, often it finds a terrible discontent, an

agonizing repulse.) If there are the buoy-
ancy and gladness of youth, so are there
the decrepitude and pathos of old age. If
there is the joy of perfect marriage, so is
there the sorrow of the widower and the
widow—or, perhaps even worse, the troub-
lous disunion of ill-mated pairs. And thus
the chain of contrast might be extended,
until we have seen that, link by link, it all
means just so much happiness for just so
much distress, just so much light for just
so much darkness.

Now, if an affectionate god is the author
of all that we term good, we cannot deny
his accountability for all that we term evil.
If he made the lily, in its chaste and odor-
ous loveliness, he made the cancer, a flower
of hideous petal and mephitic exhalation.
Nor will it serve us to affirm that all baleful things in life are the offspring of a hidden, inscrutable charity toward the race.
It is within the limit of every man's imagination to picture himself as realizing, in
some *post-mortem* state, that all afflictions
poured upon humanity have indeed been
"for the best." But even if he were then
to concede that this had been wholly true,
he could never fairly avoid the declaration
that anguish and calamity are, here and

now, persecutions and martyrdoms ruthlessly wreaked upon his living earthly kindred. He must always have that quarrel
with any god he might meet outside of the
flesh from which he has escaped. *(*To *le
grand peutêtre* he must always be ready to
present *le grand pourquoi.)* At least, he
must do so if we can speak of a disembodied soul as an entity to be dealt with by
laws of human consciousness. And how
else can we possibly deal with such an
entity?

But, on the other hand, can we deal with
it at all? Do we know, even in the vaguest
way, what the words 'a disembodied soul'
mean? They, and the melodious polysyl-
lable, 'immortality,' pass glibly enough
from the lips. A great many estimable
people are quite sure that they know precisely what is meant in the utterance of
them. But in reality these expressions are
quite wild and void. It will not do to say
that the Bible has told us what they mean,
for even admitting that the Bible be not a
book wrought by excessively ignorant and
superstitious men from material in part if
not wholly fabulous, the information which
it conveys on subjects of a supernatural
import is of no more real value than a tale

like that of Leda and the Swan or any of
the thousand myths embedded amid other
creeds. There is not the slightest reason
why we should look upon the chronicle of
either Jeremiah or St. Matthew, of either
Samuel or St. Mark, as veracious. No historian of the least real repute would, at the
present day, affirm them to be so. The
very existence of that particular Christ
whose life and death are recorded in the
New Testament is by no means a proven
fact. The ridiculous story that he was
born of a virgin is scarcely less to be respected by unbiassed judges than the story
that he was ever born at all. He is a figure not a whit more actual than Helen of
Sparta, Achilles or Hector, and the entire
legend of his crucifixion has no more historic weight than that of the siege of Troy.

But there probably was an Achilles, a
siege of Troy, and there probably was a
Christ, a crucifixion. No proof that his
Messiah was divine seems to the Christian
a stronger one than such reported words
and deeds as those of the four gospels.
Yet here are both words and deeds which
often partake rather of the anchorite's austere self-mortification and asceticism than
of the liberal and virile philanthropist's

doctrines and axioms. The character of
Christ, as his apostles depict it, is that of a
sweet-souled, pure-minded communist, yet
it is also an individuality filled with impracticable meekness and a tendency toward beautiful yet dangerous kindliness in
its dealings with the frailties, crimes and
sins of society. The best and purest of
modern Christians could not conscien-
tiously endorse the pardoning posture
shown by this Christ whom he so adores.
It is one thing to worship such an un-
flawed spirit as an ideal of mildness and
compassion ; it is another to approve meas-
ures of lowlihead and amiability which, if
carried out in the government of multitudes by an executive, would entail anarchy of the worst license. We cannot tell
hardened culprits to go and sin no more ;
they are always glad enough to "go," but
their wrongdoing is not half so easy of
dismissal. To be roughly assaulted by
some miscreant and to bid him assault
us again—to turn the other cheek toward
him after he has smitten us upon one—is
a personal revelation of self-control commendable only within the limits of Christ's
especial disposition:—that of altruistic
goodfellowship, equally wide and indulgent

But if we overlook the question of slighted self-respect, how can we approve, in this connection, a course so fatally destructive to all true social order as that of forgiveness for wrong and outrage unaccompanied by the least thought of corrective discipline and punishment? Christ, during the brief period that he is said to have appeared before men, preached a theory which would have flung open the doors of prisons and set loose upon cities and communities the most depraved desperadoes whom iron cages ever sought to detain. And this form of counsel in him his worshippers have admired as a piece of poetic abstraction alone. They have no more made it the actual rule of their lives than they have thus made the socialistic "leave all and follow me" of his other celebrated sayings.

But while agnosticism of to-day recoils from much that Christ has been accredited with stating and desiring as devoid of due dignity for the individual and without proper adhesive effect upon society at large, it still fails to see in surrounding nature even a vague confirmation of the promise which this lovely and smooth-voiced prophet so perpetually gives us of a life

after death. That wittiest and occasionally saddest of writers, Dumas the younger,
is said to have inscribed these words in the
album of a friend who solicited some sentiment over his autograph : *" L'espoir qu'à
l'homme de la vie immortelle lui vient de son
désespoir de se trouver mortel dans celui-ci."*
Here, one might say, lies the whole pith
and marrow of modern if not ancient religion. (Our despair of being mortal in
this world prompts us to fabricate for ourselves an eternal duration in some other !)
And yet the epigram of Dumas has not
touched the entire truth.   Epigrams rarely
do that ; they are fire-flies glittering in dark
places but not illuminating them, and they
show us little except their own transitory
brightness.   He neglects that impulse of
hope in every healthful human breast—
that " will to live," which is the one solid
grain of truth in Schopenhauer's and Von
Hartmann's brilliant though faulty philoso-
phies.   The vast majority of mankind cannot help believing in a future existence,
because for men not to have hope is either
to be the victim of distemper or else to
verge upon death itself. Forms of insanity
called melancholia and suicidal mania show
a complete collapse of this energy ; the

skilled physician knows well these symp-
toms in his demented patient, unless it may
be that their sudden manifestation defeats
his most wary vigilance. Yet agnosticism,
which insists upon regarding facts and re-
jecting such fanciful ghosts of them as
strut in their borrowed robes, has clearly
taught itself that our hopes of immortality
bear an exact analogous relation to our
yearnings and desires in all affairs of a
more restricted yet equally pungent kind.
Supposing that we are in a state of ordinary health, we wake at a certain hour of
the morning after a fairly restful sleep.
Our pulse is firm; our liver acts ; the machinery of vitality does not falter. Immediately, as soon as we are well awake, we
begin plans for the day, we bethink ourselves of engagements made on the day
previous, we wish to enter upon one more
diurnal routine of employment, duty and
diversion. Agnostics or Christians, we
have this same quiet, automatic longing.
And yet the extreme futility of all human
endeavor, the evanescence of all we purpose and perform, may be and often is
inexorably clear to the agnostic, while he
himself would nevertheless be the first to
admit that a strenuous force which he can-

not explain forever lifts and buoys him.
But with the ill or ailing man how different it is!) A pessimist might maintain that
the jaundiced eyes of such a man often
behold us as the masque of shadows we
really are. To his despondent brain life
will sometimes appear as arid and wearisome as a burnt prairie under a sky of
slate. The concept of an immortality for
the human soul will seem to him like some
remote conjecture born of a fanatic's
revery.

And such it really deserves to be called.
The agnostic, though he may hope to win
it or though he may prefer the nepenthean
boon of complete annihilation, sees that,
for all he can possibly learn to the contrary,
it shines the *ignis fatuus* which must perpetually evade philosophic grasp. With
wings wrought from rainbows, and eyes
from stars, it is but the intangible child of
story, song and dream. Like the κλῦθί μοι
of Homeric text, reference to it constantly
recurs on page after page of the immense
book of life. The tale of no nation could
be adequately told without it, and whenever fancy has conspired with faith to
achieve the most madcap results of illusion,
we are confronted by its Elysiums, Valhal-

las and Nirwanas. But the agnostic well
understands that the species of theological
ecstasy which has always surrounded it
conduces ill toward a proper logical sur-
vey. " Refrain," says Herbert Spencer, in
his great 'Psychology,' " from rendering
your terms into ideas, and you may reach
any conclusion whatever. ' The whole is
equal to its part ' is a proposition that may
be quite comfortably entertained, so long
as neither wholes nor parts are imagined."
It will probably be many centuries before
mankind at length abandons all belief in
immortality. Resembling not a few similar delusions, it possesses undeniable
charm, and has that sort of beauty which
the astute Mr. Lecky tells us that religious
ideas, like a dying sun, expend their last
rays in creating.

Agnosticism finds little rebuff nowadays
for its lack of conventional belief. The
pulpiteers make " infidelity " their texts,
it is true, but it takes a very ardent church-
goer, among really intelligent classes of
church-goers, not to compare the keen, lim-
pid reasoning of our modern scientific
writers with the mystic, turgid, involved
utterances of the Bible greatly to the latter's disadvantage. There is more moral

profit in half-a-dozen pages of Herbert Spencer's "Data of Ethics" or "Social Statics" than in all the statements of Paul, vague, problematic, transcendental. And yet the accusation of unmoral apathy and indifference is often brought against agnosticism. "It builds no hospitals," cry its foes ; "it endows no charities ; it is pagan in its unconcern for the sufferings of humanity. It is so occupied in sneering at Holy Writ that it forgets the sweet lessons of loving-kindness and of devotion to an unstained ideal with which those deathless leaves abound." Now, agnosticism forgets nothing of the sort, and is willing to give the New Testament credit for every line and word of sound ethics contained there, just as it is unsparing in its denunciation and disgust when asked an opinion of those crimes and horrors with which the records of the Old Testament teem, and of that bloody, vengeful Jehovah who makes up for not possessing the sensualism and lust of Jupiter by exhibiting ten times more of his deliberate cruelty and hatred. Agnosticism is very far, moreover, from the callous indifference with which it is so frequently charged. If it has not erected many charitable institutions and has headed

few eleemosynary lists, we must remember
that it has not, like Christianity, almost
two thousand years behind it. There have
been a great many lukewarm Christians,
if almsgiving is a test of the finer devoted-
ness. But already agnosticism has made,
in this respect, an excellent showing, when
we consider its youth as a modern movement—a nineteenth-century wave of tendency — apart from earlier unorthodox
growths. Professor Felix Adler has deeply and valuably interested himself in tene-
ment-house reform, and many another New
York citizen (to say nothing of those in
London) yearly gives large sums to the
poor, unstimulated by any expectation of
receiving angelic compound interest hereafter upon his earthly loan. Indeed, I
learned, not long ago, that the English
poet, Mr. William Morris, had expended a
large fortune in aiding what he believed to
be the cause of the poor against the rich. Mr.
Morris's motives may be declared socialistic rather than simply and humanely generous; but they nevertheless afford one
more instance of a rationalist and freethinker who does not live in selfish disregard of his fellow-men. In fact this fling
at agnosticism as being so cold-blooded-

ly epicurean resembles the absurd rumors
which were set afloat after the deaths of
Voltaire and Thomas Paine. It is probable that these two famous infidels died
very much the same as ordinary mortals
die, though a few random, delirious mur-
murs may have been readily misinterpreted
by partisan listeners. Not long ago we
had occasion to see with what sweet and
sublime courage a freethinker could
breathe his last, when Courtlandt Palmer
summoned wife and children to his bedside
and addressed them in words full of the
gentlest and most fearless tranquillity.
And yet if Palmer's mind had wandered,
at the last, and some grisly hallucination
had chanced to usurp it, how probable that
there would have been somebody—a servant,
perhaps, or one of the country-folk in that
quiet Vermont retreat where his death oc-
curred—who would have asserted monstrous things about his final "remorseful
agonies"!

As for charitable inclination on the part
of agnosticism, it is just as certain to augment with increasing years as frigid ava-
rice is certain to develop. There was never
a more preposterous statement than that
the religion of Christ brought humanita-

rianism into the world. Man's pity for his
fellow-man existed a thousand years previously in India, where hospitals were
among the comforts of civilization.. Very
possibly the standard of physical health in
Greece and Rome was far above ours, and
hence hospitals were not required in either
nation. If it were true, as so often has
been affirmed, that the Romans exposed
their old people to die on an island in the
Tiber, then such action (grossly inconsist-
ent with the splendid morality of the race
previous to its downfall) must be explained
as the deed perpetrated by a clique rather
than a class—and a most depraved and
vagabond one at that. And even in the
latter case these exposed persons were
probably slaves. Both Rome and Greece,
the countries that produced Cæsar and
Themistocles, Cicero and Aristotle, were
cursed by slavery. So was the United
States, until a few years ago. Who shall
presume to say that in this highly Christian country cruelties have not taken place
that might bring envious glitters into the
eyes of a Caligula ? And if agnosticism had
been a prevailing characteristic of the
populace south of Mason and Dixon's line,
how easy to have held it blamable for the

brutalities of the whipping-post, the drunk-
en overseer, the hideous auction and the
pursuant bloodhound !   In the days of
their real glory Greece and Rome were
marked by a phenomenal refinement and
a *morale* of surpassing integrity.   Christianity, which may be said to have bathed
Europe in bloodshed, brought also the impassioned zealot with his dreams of heavenly bliss and the martyr with his unflinch-
ing gaze at the fagots which were to con-
sume him.   But there are no grander examples in mediæval times of unswerving
adherence to duty at the price of absolute
self-sacrifice and self-immolation than those
given us in ancient times by such men as
Brutus and Virginius.   And if agnosticism
should wish to point toward a man of un-
paralleled probity, consistency and bravery
as its representative, what figure could
more sufficiently stand for these qualities
than that intrepid and picturesque one
of Giordano Bruno ?   When we consider
the superb intellectual heights which were
attained by Athens, how nonsensical seems
the claim that Christianity bore civilization in its wake, or that what we call
European civilization was anything except
that evolutional result of cerebral and

climatic conditions indicated so compe-
tently by Buckle, Draper and writers of
their forceful calibre ! (Full as many sins
as virtues have been committed in the name
of the Cross. The Inquisition, the Massacre
of St. Bartholomew, the slaughter of the
Albigenses, the appalling persecutions of
the Jews, all should now belong to the very
alphabet of juvenile instruction. But alas !
it is not every child who is permitted to
profit by such historic truths in their candid nakedness. ·Happily, the children of
agnostics are always allowed this privilege.

A novel which has for many months
been occupying the attention of English
and American readers, presumably has
won its great vogue from the challenge
which its charming though not profound
pages have cast at agnosticism. There
are few more entertaining stories than
" Robert Elsmere," and if it were a trifle
more chiselled in style than it already is, it
might easily take rank among the masterpieces of fiction. This is said, however,
purely from the literary standpoint ; from
the standpoint of sincere and valid thinking it is a work narrow with all the peculiar and " trimming" narrowness of the late
Matthew Arnold, whose influence has been

diffused through its pages and who easily shows himself as the Mentor of its creative Telemachus. Robert Elsmere is a noble and lovable being, and one plainly meant by the author to express liberalism and large-mindedness at the very last limit of their admissible extension. But Mrs. Ward, like her kinsman and posthumous coadjutor, Matthew Arnold, halts at a point plainly within the bounds of conventional thought. Elsmere, though trained as an English clergyman, gives up his living because a belief in the "divinity" of Christ has become to him a void and sham. But instead of allowing full play to his rich gifts of fellowship and helpfulness without further concern for the ghost-worship from which he should now be happily freed, we find him building a new faith upon the ruins of the old. Unitarianism has always been one of the drollest of compromises between Christianity and agnosticism; and although Elsmere does not attempt to walk on this curious bridge that joins two such widely different banks, he nevertheless clearly avoids that boldness and justice of mental demeanor which might have been expected from a man of both his native and cultivated equipments. Mr. Huxley says :

" If a man asks me what the politics of the inhabitants of the moon are, and I reply that I do not know, that neither I nor anyone else have any means of knowing, and that under these circumstances I decline to trouble myself about the subject, I do not think he has any right to call me a skeptic." Robert Elsmere might with consistency and excellent common-sense have taken a stand like this. Yet no ; he had renounced Christ, but he must still concern himself with—the politics of the inhabitants of the moon. Precisely as Matthew Arnold was forever doing, he personifies all the good in the world with an actual wantonness of unfortified assumption, calls it by the name of God and insists upon paying it reverence.

There is, Matthew Arnold long ago declared, a " power not ourselves which makes for righteousness," and it has always seemed to me that just such enemies as this talented and facile writer are at once the most polite and most irritating of any with whom agnosticism is called upon to deal. Matthew Arnold belonged to that type of essayist and controversialist who is wrecked and enfeebled by the very "culture" of which he is so impas-

sioned a convert. He diluted his own abilities into feebleness by mixing them with
dilettanteism. It might be said of him
that his future fame, unlike Keats's, has
been written not so much in water as in
Arnold-and-water. Born under the Oxon-
ian shadow of episcopacy, possessing a
father whom his " Literature and Dogma"
must have struck as the riot and carnival
of heterodoxy, Matthew Arnold was never
able to welcome those honest doubts which
his own width of intellect had summoned.
The age forced him to weigh, to sift, to
investigate reverend things ; but he did so
à contre cœur, and always with vivid mem-
ories of how his youth had treasured their
sacredness. Agnosticism, pure and simple, had for him a violence of emphasis
that set his teeth on edge. It was extremely unfortunate for the gentleman's
teeth—rather more so than for agnosticism. He was a man born either too early
or too late. Perhaps it had best be said of
him that he was born too late, for, taking
him all in all, he would have made a much
better Church of England dignitary than
the agnostic he is sometimes incorrectly
called.

To state that there is a "power not our-

selves which makes for righteousness" is to
postulate the undemonstrable. It has always been the favorite method of Matthew
Arnold and men who resemble him, to let
sentiment pose on the pedestals of their
overthrown gods. If there be such a
power, what is it? Does it really exist
outside the consciousness of man? If so,
can its existence be proven, or partly
proven, or even vaguely revealed? Provided
my neighbor and I choose to live an up-
right and sinless life, what is the power
not ourselves that leads us to do so? Is not
the power essentially of and in ourselves?
Is it not a result of our respective relation-
ships with the men and women around us?
Imagine that the planet contained but a
single human being, and lo, the moral or
unmoral acts that he could commit would
be reduced to almost a minimum! Even
suicide would not be criminal, for in putting an end to his solitary life this lone
creature would wound no kinsman or friend,
he would break no dear ties, deal grief to no
loving hearts, bring shame upon no house
or clan. But give this lonely denizen of
earth a single companion, and at once new
moral and unmoral conditions arise. Say
that his companion is feminine, and that the

Adam who now finds himself in the society
of an Eve is called upon to perform a hundred little acts of protective kindliness
which she in turn reciprocates by gentle
sympathies peculiar to her sex. Of necessity a new order of moral conduct has
been established. There are acts good and
evil which this pair can mutually wreak
upon one another. And then, if we in-
crease our duo by one, two, three, or say
ten individuals, how complicated the relations will become! We have the beginning of a society ; and in a society all virtue and all wrongdoing must depend upon
the aidful or deterrent relations between
its members.

Here, then, is where the pseudo-liberalism
of such thinkers as Matthew Arnold, after
leaving the beaten path of Christianity,
swings back to its monotheism and its
pietism by another route. This is what
Robert Elsmere does in the engaging novel
of that name. He confuses his desire for
a celestial and infinite Friend (whom he
has accepted in the place of a lost Christ)
with the meagre and insufficient proofs
afforded by nature and all ethnologic
history that any such occult potency lives
outside of space and time. Other men as

brave and fine as he have had the same desire and yet have separated it from the perceptive push of their brains as they would winnow chaff from wheat. Experience is forever teaching us that the gulf between what we want and what we get here below the visiting moon is indeed abysmal. Into that abyss the real agnostic unflinchingly gazes. Elsmere had so gazed as well, but had grown foolishly fascinated by the bodiless and tricksy sprites that seemed to float' through its uncharted vacuum.

An objection often made to agnosticism by persons of penetration and scholarship is that it destroys without replacing, and that he only destroys who can replace. In other words, religion, as these excellent people claim, is mutable but ineradicable ; you cannot take it away from the human race in one form without substituting it in another. Worship has always been and will always be. Agnosticism is not worship, but simply negation. It can never satisfy the cravings of mortality ; it can never be made to stand for the rolling organ, the stately altar, the chanted hymn, the curling incense, the prayerful genuflection. . . . Now, the truth is, all such dissent

is founded upon a single error—that of supposing mankind has any natural tendency
to worship at all.   In his barbarous conditions his worship is grovelling, and shows
clearly the terrorism which has induced it.
Afterward fear changes to awe, and with
many impressionable persons (these being
chiefly women) a kind of love is generated,
perfervid, idolatrous, tinged by hysteria.
But let us imagine that all religious people in the world could to-morrow become
absolutely certain this god whom they
venerate was himself but a portion of nature,
subject to its laws and powerless to alter
them by the least fraction of an infringe-
ment.   What would then result?   Would
not all this zealous 'love' depart on the
instant?   Would not the monk slip off his
shirt of serge, and the nun forego her fasts?

'God is love,' say the churchmen.   It
would be equally true, judging from what
life shows us, to declare that 'God is hate.'
But truer than either would it be to maintain that 'God is fear.'   We cannot really
love an incorporeal dream, a fantasy im-
palpable as moonlight.   We may love the
idea of loving it, and cultivate in ourselves
that delicate or robust sort of frenzy which
is to all religion what its greenness is to a

leaf; but the effort of evolution is rather to produce in man a complete discontinuance of prostration before unknowable finalities. A man's home is all the church he needs. Wife and children make charming choristers and acolytes. He can find plenty of spiritual elevation, if so disposed, in ministering to the needs and comforts of his fellows. There is more merit and import in one charitable act than in the hallelujahs and hosannas of a mighty concourse. Prayer is merely a refinement of fetishism. Herbert Spencer says that volumes could be written on the impiety of the pious ; he might have added that volumes could also be written on the idiocy of prayer. To call god omniscient, omnipotent, an all-loving and all-merciful father, one moment, and the next, perhaps, implore him to save a treasured child in the agonies of croup or meningitis—who is there that does not see the mockery of such a contradiction ?

It would be hard to conceive of a more peaceful state of things for the world at large than that which would result from a cessation to think at all concerning the unknowable and the beginning to accept some pantheistic creed like Spinoza's. Incessant dread of what may be the life to come has

often caused neglect of the concerns and
demands of life here.   If we knew to-morrow for a certainty that death meant an
eternal falling asleep, we should doubtless
busy ourselves much more than we do with
that term of wakefulness allotted to us.
As John Stuart Mill has most tellingly said,
there is horror in the idea of dying, solely
because our minds insist upon fancying
that we should continue conscious after
ceasing to breathe—as if any such phase
were possible as that of *being dead!*   Of
course the actuality of death as a dark
human ill could never be argued away.   It
is not so much that we feel the *ego* decay-
ing, weakening, and at last ending, as that
we are doomed before our own demise to
look on those whom we love or admire
while they fade before our sight.   Death,
howsoever we rationally consider it, is a
curse, not alone because it visits us in
countless ghastly shapes and because we
are never sure what fierce sufferings its
visits will entail, but because it constantly
tears from us those whom we love under
circumstances of the most immature and
ill-timed quality.   If we could all live to be
so old that death would affect us as extreme ripeness affects a fruit, causing it to

drop from its bough after completing a
period of progressive and harmonious
thrift, the dolor and exaction would be far
less apparent. But even then *pallida mors*
would not be stripped of its worst repul-
sion, for there are many old people who
yet cling to life after senility has brought
them its deepest wrinkles, its most halting
footsteps. "Live sanely," say the hygien-
ists, "and you will die happily." (But this
counsel is the most fallible of apothegms,
for there are thousands who must live not
only in the sanest way but with the rigid-
est self-denial in order to live at all, because of inherited maladies.) Even agnostics will sometimes tell you that perpetual
life on this planet would be wearisome to
them ; but what man or woman could will
to die if health and the companionship of
a few loved ones were vouchsafed him ? To
live on like Zanoni or the Wandering Jew
would indeed prove a torment ; but provided certain dear existences could be
healthfully and vigorously prolonged together with our own, what paradise ever
sketched by the most dazzling poetic fancy
could equal the loveliness of this orb in
which we now dwell ? Harsh winters may
prevail upon certain tracts of it ; angry

tempests may pour their liquid and electric rage upon it ; the tumbling domains of its ocean may abound with shipwreck ; heat may often parch its meadows, and drouth may turn its rivers to arid hollows of sand; but the glorious beauty of our planet, its charms of rock, sea, field, foliage, landscape, are an unending consolement and delight. The extraordinary reputed visions of John in the isle of Patmos are as nothing to it, nor could our intelligence evolve any conceivable picture in which both colors and lines, howsoever newly commingled, are not borrowed from its own. No ; immortality here on earth, under the circumstances just named, could not well fail of enjoyment. The very persons who now shudder at the prospect of its ennui would hardly fail to choose it if given a chance. At any rate, dismay might result to anyone who counted too rashly upon the certainty of their refusal.

Say that some youth were brought up in absolute ignorance of all the bitterness and melancholy with which religion has associated death. Let us suppose that he had grown to regard death simply as a tender peace, a blessed rest after toil, a slumber which indeed "knits up the ravell'd sleave

of care." Then say that sudden tidings
came to him, at the age of twenty or there-
abouts, which entirely upset all his former
deductions. Thus far, perhaps, he had
seen a parent or a sister die. (Pain had
preceded dissolution, making its ultimate
repose all the more grateful, and he had
joined with others in the relief that such
emancipation and exemption produced.
But now, abruptly, he learns of the fright-
ful things that man has been for many
years believing about death. The ghastli-
ness of Hell, the forlornness of Purgatory,
and the tedium of an interminable Heaven
all rise before him. Orthodoxy seizes
him by one hand, bigotry by the other,
and no wonder if he recoils terrified, disgusted, from the contact of each. It would
not be strange if he were to go mad from
the shock of his discovery, provided he
became a convert to any of the creeds it
has laid bare. After years of entire mental
calm he has been beset by turmoil and
vexation. Agnosticism is his only refuge,
and if he takes it he may there find at
least a similitude of the contentment he
knew before.

Of course this instance is only a supposi-
titious one. But the imagination can easily

deal with it, and it might be real enough were any human being educated like the individual whom I have fancied. Agnosticism would sponge the slate clean, and thus wipe away every past impression and prejudice. To state that it must replace what it has destroyed is idle verbiage, for to require that it shall replace one superstition by another would mean that it should bring the recurrence of captivity instead of a new and unique liberation. If I tell my friend that he has in his pocket a counterfeit banknote I am not compelled to give him genuine money as the price of my news. The great mistake of those who condemn and oppose agnosticism is their stubborn insistence that it shall build some sort of new church, establish some sort of new priesthood. This mistake is natural enough, and quite pardonable considering its source. Agnosticism pretends to be nothing in the way of a new religion; you might as well ask it to explain itself as ask the sunshine that pierces a cloud-swathed sky after days of gloom and storm. It is the reasoning faculty of humanity grown an assertion instead of an abnegation, a sound instead of a silence, a courage instead of a cowardice. Such writers as Mr.

Frederic Harrison, Mr. W. H. Mallock, and others of either a sentimental or an infatuated turn, wholly fail to comprehend that the sense of being free from all codes and restrictions invented by human credulity alone, is at once exhilarant and fortifying. It may be said that certain minds cannot do without the religions of churches ; if so, there is no objection to the possessors of these minds continuing to thumb prayer-books. But others of hardier mould, of firmer fibre, will prefer the one large republic of rationalism to the little monarchies and duchies of orthodoxy. Professor Huxley has well called this latter " the Bourbon of thought." And he adds : " It learns not, neither can it forget; and though at present bewildered and afraid to move, it is as willing as ever to insist that the first chapter of Genesis contains the beginning and the end of sound science, and to visit with such petty thunderbolts as its half-paralyzed hands can hurl those who refuse to degrade nature to the level of primitive Judaism."

We near the birth of a new century, and it may be true that before the world is a hundred years older marvellous effects will have accrued from the persistent and

undaunted efforts of science. Possibly
agnosticism will then almost have changed
into a certain kind of gnosticism ; before
many more centuries have elapsed we are
led to trust that it will surely have so
changed. If the denizens of Mars were
actually signalling to us, as that Italian
astronomer is reported not long ago to
have claimed that they are, and if anything
like interplanetary communication were
established between Mars and ourselves,
this event would really be no more extraordinary than others brought about by men
like Newton, Franklin, Fulton or Edison.
If our descendants master the secret of
death and wring immortality from nature,
these acts will be only analogous to what
man is already doing. Toward such a
millennial result every loyal agnostic will
have given his share. (He who has lifted
but a single stone of it still helps to build
the pyramid. What a debt do we owe to
the ancestors that freed us from superstition's trammelling tyrannies ! A like debt
will our successors owe to us in the ages
unborn. This realization must content the
agnostic. It is a lofty one, and it is
chastely unselfish as well. He cannot say
that he has no good cause for thanks ; he

has been saved from temporizing and makeshift ; he has escaped the silliness of Theosophy, "Christian Science," "spirit-ualism," and like tawdry lures to the fancy and the senses ; he has stooped his lips to the crystal waters of pure knowledge and found there a draught far wholesomer and more flavorous than any sacramental wine ever served by foolish priests !

Agnosticism, it might be said, kneels before a mighty door, in whose huge lock is a massive, rusted key. Year after year she bruises her hands trying to turn the key ; again and again she has moved it a little—but only a little, always. She does not know what lies beyond the door ; she does not profess, she does not even ask, to know. But it is the door of human life, and beyond it is infinity. Though her hands are crimson with blood and their flesh is torn to the bone, she will never desist from her task. She may faint for a time, but she will not die, for her other name is Truth-Seeker, and that means imperishability. And now and then, while she strives with all her power to turn the monstrous key, her teeth will clench themselves and she will defiantly murmur : "Not if it takes ten thousand years will I ever

cease to struggle, until the key has been
swung round in its lock and the door has
been flung open!"

She does not grow old with the years,
either, this obstinate Agnosticism. Time
brings her strength instead of. weakness,
and though she is very old she is yet
younger to-day than in the period of
Lucretius. Will she fail in her supreme
design? It may be. But no matter; she
will have striven !

THE ARROGANCE OF OPTIMISM.

NOT very long ago the present writer had
occasion to examine a criticism in the *New
York Times* which-dealt with a recent novel
by Mr. Edgar Saltus. This novel, as many
readers will remember, had attracted attention because of its chiselled phrases
and diamond-like epigram. It was not,
however, a book which might be expected
to please everybody, and perhaps its young
author was far from anticipating that it
would. But possibly, on the other hand,
he was not prepared to hear, as the acid
newspaper critic soon informed him, that
he had been presenting "in an ugly bou-
quet the poison-weeds that Schopenhauer
and Von Hartmann cultivated." And then,
almost immediately afterward, this implacable person went on to declare that Mr.
Saltus was "imbued with the most horrible of all human dementia," and that he

had written a work which, "as a romance, drips pessimism."

Such assertions as these are beginning to have a very old ring. It is now a good, appreciable length of time since the genuine agnostic was successfully pulverized by the wrathful pulpiteer. He is not pulverized any more; occasionally he is shrieked at after the style of Mr. Talmage, whose well-known energy in this capacity has long ago become for thousands an amusement as purely national as that of base-ball or roller-skating. Still, the agnostic and the pessimist are not by any means necessarily one. The agnostic may be, and not infrequently is, an optimist of sunny and even roseate outlook. He will tell you that because the roots of all earthly progress are wrapped in obscurity, and because the goal toward which the mighty steps of evolution advance is veiled by unknowableness, that is no reason for despair of the "one far-off divine event" which Tennyson's verses have prophesied so beautifully. He may even inform you of how his own religious uncertainty and insecurity do not forbid him to hope, trust, and at times feel almost confident that the entire vast system of the universe is governed by an intelligence wholly

beneficent and gracious—one whose apparently cruel deeds are disguised mercies
and whose seeming enmity hides a love
which our future immortality shall both
comprehend and applaud. The modern
agnostic has a logical and consistent right
to this attitude if he can sincerely assume
it. But he has not the right to treat with
arrogance the opposite views aud opinions
of the pessimist, nor is he often found in
the employment of any such mischievous
and ill-advised tactics. All that he leaves
for the religionists, the orthodox believers,
the zealots of a "revealed" faith. And it
must be admitted that even in this age of
toleration the poor pessimist has a rather
unpopular and dreary time of it. A rat set
upon by a terrier might expect about as
much sympathy from unmerciful bystand-
ers as he receives from the majority of his
contemporaries. A great many sensible
men dismiss his creed with a sneer as silly
in the extreme ; it is no less a triviality to
them than theosophy would be to Mr. Huxley or spiritualism to Mr. Lecky. A great
many good and sensible women turn from
it with a shudder as "hopeless," "despairing," and "sinful." An enormous number
of ignorant or half-educated people, if they

regard it at all, do so with contemptuous aversion. Then there are those of all classes who insist that the pessimist does not believe what he professes to believe—that he is attitudinizing, posing, and that everybody ought to *faire son possible* in the way of frowning him out of such folly. These methods of treatment, when considered without prejudice or bias of any sort, are best defined by a single word—arrogance. They savor of precisely the same spirit as that which was manifested, only a few years ago, toward everybody who presumed to doubt the inspiration of Scripture. Nowadays a man can be an agnostic with some degree of mundane comfort, but the lot of the pessimist has not yet been similarly favored. I have observed that his greatest enemy, as in the case of Mr. Saltus, is the newspaper. This exults in having its fling at the writer or thinker who dares to "look on the dark sides of things" or to "don green spectacles"—both of which idioms flow from the editorialist's pen with a glibness that bespeaks long practice in their use. It is an easy matter, surely, to write down anything in this way, from a political measure to a pot of Récamier Cream, from an execution by electricity to a new Gilbert-and-Sullivan opera. Very probably, too, the current newspaper has one of its innumerable self-preservative "policies " to uphold, since it would never do for the average citizen so sharply to realize the complete nothingness of things that he cared no longer for his morning and evening journal. And yet the point-of-view taken in every cited instance is an arrogant one. Expediency may prompt, very often, the crushing blows aimed at a gloomy system of philosophy; for there are many people in the world foolish enough to doubt whether the naked truth should ever be looked on by mortality provided its limbs are graceless and its tinges repelling. But by far the larger part of these antago-nists whom I have mentioned consider themselves in duty bound to discounte-nance uncheerful tenets. It is right and godly that they should do so ; it would be arrant wickedness to behave otherwise than as the wagers of a vigorous crusade against such vicious notions. "Bah ! Stuff and nonsense !" cries irritated society. "This world not a pleasant place to live in ? Mankind had far better not have been born ? Go, preach your rubbish to the 'cranks' that are not above listening to it!"

All of which has, when coming from the lips of society, a truly impressive sound. That is, at first.   But a little later we might find ourselves reflecting that society has had a fashion of being obstinately unconvinced, as regarded the greatest and most vital questions, for a period of several thousand years.   All history, it might be stated, is only a vast record of the mistakes made by the masses.   Naturally those preachers who succeed in getting the hugest multitudes to hear them are not merely such as thrill their listeners with promises of an abundant and beatific immortality, but who embellish the vistas of that fortunate prospect with a most lavish charm of ornamentation.   It might be said of the big public, indeed, that such persons as the Rev. Dr. Talmage have spoiled them for ordinary theological treatment : they are no longer satisfied unless their immortality is served them, so to speak, with a thick layer of icing and a good many plums.   Here is the sort of pungent encouragement they need, and the paragraphs containing it are quoted from a sermon delivered by the gentleman already named :

"*Friends, the exit from this world, or death, if you please to call it, to the Christian is glo-*

rious expectation. It is demonstration. It is illumination. It is sunburst. It is the opening of all the windows. It is shutting up the cate- chism of doubt, and the unrolling of all the scrolls of positive and accurate information. . . . It is the last mystery taken out of botany and astrono- my and geology. O, will it not be grand to have all questions answered! . . . The Bible intimates that we will talk with Jesus in heaven just as a brother talks with a brother. Now, what will you ask him first? . . . I shall first want to hear the tragedy of his last hours, and then Luke's account of the crucifixion and then Mark's account of the crucifixion and John's account of the crucifixion will be nothing, while from the living lips of Christ the story shall be told of the gloom that fell, and the devils that arose. . . . All heaven will stop to listen until the story is done, and every harp will be put down, and every lip closed, and all eyes fixed on the Divine narrator, until the story is done ; and then, at the tap of the bâton, the eternal orchestra will rouse up; finger on string of harp, and lips to the mouth of trumpet, there shall roll forth the oratorio of the Messiah."

If there were any refined or cultivated people who took this kind of flamboyant materialism at all seriously, they might be pardoned for feeling that an eternity of such proceedings would prove quite the reverse of celestial. But that people with no refinement or cultivation should discover latent "comfort" in talk of so entirely whimsical a character only serves to illustrate what a particularly small minority of votes the pessimistic person could ever be able to command. On every side he would seem to have the inherent *gaietĕ dĕ cœur* of humanity against him. This condition of affairs, let it once more be pointed out, clearly exhibits the arrogance of optimism. What that tendency wills to believe, it does believe. It refuses to think that life is not worth living, and it thus refuses in the face of myriad facts indicated by the rigid and unerring finger of science. No assertion is made that this arrogance is one just now to be avoided or lived down ; it may, in fact, be inseparable from the race as thus far evolved, and constitute that very "will to live" without which, as Schopenhauer asserts, there would be no organic or even inorganic existence whatever. But viewed from the standpoint of him who opposes it determinedly, it is arrogance, nevertheless. For while the pessimist can give countless proofs that life is a curse, a snare, a bewilderment, a disappointment, an affliction, the optimist can give no correspondingly valid proofs to the contrary. No design is now proposed either to endorse or condemn optimism, but merely to define it. The optimist may say, and veraciously enough, that under given conditions of happiness or contentment he holds life to be amply worth living. But the pessimist refuses to deal solely with those conditions. He insists upon looking at life as altogether an impersonal, un-individual affair. He weighs its aggregate of unsolicited misery against its aggregate of reaped and garnered joy, and concludes that the former far outbalances the latter.

The pessimist, in his purely unemotional rôle of scientist, can no more be despised than any other dispassionate taker of statistics. If he shouts anathemas against the optimist he at once ranks himself among the great throng of inexact and therefore untrustworthy thinkers. He must either be rational and credible or he swiftly becomes absurd. He has already been called absurd by legions of alert detractors. Can he prove that such vilifiers are mendacious? What are his real *renseignements?* In which avenue of reputable thought or philosophy can he find his hardy allies of argument?

He will answer you, if he be a pessimist of unblemished and invulnerable honesty, that he finds every known aid in the vivid, austere rank-and-file of human experience. "I am not a believer in any 'revealed' religion," he will tell you. "I set my Bible and my Koran on the same shelf of my library, and if the slightest patrician difference exists between their separate bindings, that is a question which entirely refers itself to the orthodoxy or the liberalism of my bookseller. I observe life with an attentive but unbiassed gaze."

"And you see in life," instantly responds the adverse auditor, "innumerable pleasures, benefits, blessings, mercies. You cannot deny this. You say that life is not worth living, and yet you, this particular pessimist whom I now address,* are rich in worldly goods, unassailed as to reputation, possessed of a wife who not merely adores you but who piques your vanity enjoyably by being the favorite of all whom she meets. You have children who are

---

* A prosperous member of society is here intentionally specified.

straight and tall and beautiful, and who
look on the heaviest task as merest leis-
ure provided you approve its onus and its
discipline. Your friends group about you
and esteem you. You breakfast with discretion ; you sup with sanity. You have
learned long ago the wisdom of abstemiousness; you are the despair of your family
physician, whose fat income of dollars can
secure no augment from your exasperat-
ing prudence. The worn and hackneyed
interrogatory of *cui bono* has no meaning
for your ears ; you live without a misfortune ; your very sleep is undisturbed by
even so much as an agreeable dream.
Your exemption from an hour, a minute
of distemper, weakness, indisposition, is
not the least of all these favors. Can
you truthfully tell me that simply with
such complete freedom from all physical aches and pains you do not congratu-
late yourself on being the possessor of a
human existence ? Can you truthfully assert that you would rather not have been at
all than be as you are ? Nullity, non-existence, is, I admit, inconceivable to human
consciousness in a subjective way. If you
had never been born you would never have
known even the peaceful serenity of not

having breathed ; you would simply have
been (if one may presume to say it) a
minus quantity in the enormous equation
of our terrestrial algebra. But *would you
have preferred* extinction to your present
sojourn upon the planet named Earth?
Are not the loves you have felt worth loving? Is not the music you have heard
worth hearing? Are not the paintings and
sculptures you have seen worth seeing?
Have not the numberless complexities of
human character with which circumstance
has associated you been worth exploring
and scrutinizing? Plainly, candidly, as
man to man, do you not think the whole
problem of life has been one which you
would have chosen to confront, provided
you had been a naked spirit on the borders
between chaos and order, with volition
enough to decide between annihilation or
creation, consciousness or cerebral blank?"

"I grant all that you say," answers the
pessimist thus directly addressed. "I am
a happy husband, a happy father; I am
the possessor of wealth ; all the pleasures
that environment may bestow upon me are
mine. My heart beats with an equal stroke ;
my digestion waits on appetite ; I have my
book-shelves lined with the masterpieces in

literature of the immortal dead ; I cannot complain that I have been visited with a single ill of the many to which flesh is heir. And yet I am miserable. I do not accept life ; it has been forced upon me. I go to my bed, I awake from my repose, with one immitigable sensation—despair."

"But why do you despair?" comes the query.

"Why? Can you ask me? I am under a rigid death-sentence. It is true that all my human encompassment shares the same bitter doom of threat. But that is no comfort to me. If I had been a condemned prisoner waiting for execution it would afford me no solace that hundreds of others near me had been similarly treated. Immortality? I know nothing about it. You tell me that a certain book, written centuries ago, abounds in hope and assurance of it. But I reject the evidence of that book. I cannot admit that it is divinely inspired. I know that a man named Polycarp said that it was, and another man named Eusebius, and another man named Irenæus. But I reject the evidence of these witnesses. They were born in an age that was balefully fertile in the most odious of superstitions. (I have only the frailest of proofs

that even such a man as Jesus Christ ever
existed. But if he did exist I can gain no
consolation from legendary statement that
he was the son of a benign overruling
deity.) You speak of the happiness that is
afforded me by the society of my wife. It
is true that I adore her—that every linea-
ment of her visage, every curve of her form,
is unspeakably dear to me. And yet I have
never known the untrammelled delight of
loving her for the sweet, winsome woman
she is. My adoration for her has ever been
mingled with terror. I mean the terror of
losing her. You, an optimist, would declare this an 'unhealthy' mood. You
would affirm it to be the 'borrowing of
trouble.' Easy phrases, my friend! And
yet I have lain awake at night with the beloved form of my wife near me, and shud-
dered at the thought of my awful solitude
if death should rid me of her priceless
company! You remonstrate with me, you
of the sunny mind, the imperishable optimism. 'Why,' you ask, 'should I dream
of horrors where none are to be found?'
Yet pause, my genial-souled friend. A
month ago my next-door neighbor would
stop me in the street to clasp my hand
with eager amity. He was the picture

of ruggedness then—only a month ago!
In his cheek health blushed, in his eye
health kindled. His wife, who worshipped
him, had said to me : 'I am so happy because my husband has no ailment, because
he is unharmed by the least bodily ill.'
...Yesterday I saw that wife. Her attire
was one blackness of mourning. Her
lip trembled as I took her hand. Life
to her had suddenly become a torture.
Why should it not so become to me, at any
hour, at any instant? I fold my arms all
the closer about my own wife in realizing
the possibility of a like calamity ; but my
love is none the less mingled with fear.
What should I do if she were torn from
me ? Could I take up again the burden of
living ? No, no ; as I watch her live face it.
seems impossible that she should be made
mute and irresponsive to this devotion I
hoard for her, inexhaustible, the sweet
miserly accrument of conjugal years ! And
my children ! How I love *them !* They are
she ; they are even more ; the guileless
egotism of fatherhood invests their treasured vitality. I press my lips to my daughter's lips, to the lips of my son, with a
passion different from yet even more sacred
than the ecstasy of manhood's early love.

And yet they, my children, are menaced
by the same dreadful threat! Yesterday
Agnes told me that her heart pulsated too
rapidly; I placed my hand upon her bosom
with a sense of unspeakable anxiety.
Yesterday Harold said to me, 'Father, I
have a headache.' My touch upon his
brow seemed so cold to myself that I feared
lest he might shrink from it. 'Idle self-
tormentings!' cry you, my optimist friend.
And yet we both know that Nature is
pitiless. My love for my offspring is not so
large—immeasurable though I feel it!—
as the deadly ambuscaded forces of ever-
watchful, ever-treacherous death! My Agnes, my Harold, are well; my worriment
was nonsense. Oh, yes, I admit it...but
a coffin was lately carried out of a house
in the next street to mine, and in it lay a
youth of Harold's age, smitten by pneumonia. A few streets further away there
was another funeral last week; a young
girl, just the age of my Agnes, had died of
diphtheria. Oh, it is all mere 'croaking'
to speak as I speak now. But what may a
human soul do with all its love if it cannot
be the guardian and warder of that love's
perpetuity? I tell myself that I should go
mad if I lost my wife or my son or my

daughter. And yet others, on every side of me, survive disasters as keen and stringent. Perhaps I would survive them, too ...I don't know...I only know that I would infinitely have preferred not being born into this world at all than being born into it with the dear, sweet weight and burden of what I now must bear! Are the joy and satisfaction of possessing kindred as treasured as my own commensurate with the stern and persevering fear of their possible loss? I answer, No. And I answer it not only from the depths of my intellect but from the depths of my love!"

How can the optimist answer a plaint like this? He cannot rationally assert that the pessimist puts forward one illogical claim. He may laugh with as blithe a mirth as Hebe's at the fabled banquets of Jove. He may point to the sun and revel in its golden ardors. But he must accede that night follows, howsoever the jubilance and splendor of day may tarry. The arrogance of optimism must at certain times make itself felt to him, even though he denies that it has been exerted. He, like the pessimist, has loved ones. The stealthy and irreversible advance of age cannot be disputed by him. He does not grow old

half so gracefully as he professes to do.
His hair does not turn into the sarcastic
silver of decay, his limbs do not secrete a
subtle chalk in their joints, his forehead
does not develop the immedicable wrinkles
and crow's-feet, his teeth do not turn ache-
haunted and loose, without his knowledge
and sure comprehension of such piteous
disintegration.   He may "philosophize";
he may don a bold front against the gradual, loitering advance of the sure destroyer ;
and yet in his inmost heart he recognizes
and bitterly appreciates the slow, terrible
change.

There is some uplifting force, affirms the
disciple of Schopenhauer, which enables
us to eat our daily meals (provided we are
among the limited though fortunate number of those who can procure them) and
bear a comparatively stout heart along with
us during the brief passage between cradle
and grave. What, you ask, is that peculiar
undemonstrated force ?   "It is," the Scho-
penhauerite will answer you, "'the will to
live,' the undeniable yet mysterious influence that equally causes a violet to spring
up by the side of a brook and Saturn to
wheel his awful globe about the sun."

"Not so," affirms the Christian, "it is

God, conscious and supremely intelligent,
ordering His universe with unrivalled wisdom and ability." The Christian and optimist are, in this case, supposed to be one
and the same, though many Christians exist who are thorough pessimists at heart,
fighting for dogma with an invincible stub-
bornness, yet ruling their lives by principles
and doctrines which the Galilean would
have held forlornly foolish. But the real
pessimist will not for a moment hear that
the least proof of intelligence is to be found
among the workings of Nature. " My great
reason," he will tell you, "for holding existence to be a curse and a bore, is my firm
conviction that we are, all of us, the mere
puppets of some sightless and wholly mind-
less Process, which moves us, not whithersoever it will, but whithersoever it must.
You assure me that above all things there
is a presiding and prevailing Consciousness.
But I have no such certainty, and the creed
to which I cling is in thousands of ways
more tenable than yours. You affect to
despise me in the arrogance of your optimism, and you hurl sentences of Scripture at
me, such as ' The fool hath said in his heart,
There is no God.' But I am not to be dis-
missed half so easily as that. My doubts

will *return to haunt you* at many future hours
of your life, even though you now profess
so valiantly to despise them.   For this
faith of yours in the complete mercy of your
God I fail to find half as thorough as you
yourself would have me think it.   The
arms of optimists like you are not torn away
any the more easily, I have observed, from
the forms of their beloved dead because of
that 'corruptible' which 'must put on in-
corruption' or that 'house not made with
hands, eternal in the heavens.'   Your sobs,
at times like these, echo none the less
drearily than those wrung from the lips of
the unbelieving.   You say that the intense
physical alteration brought about by death
is sufficient to create in you this horror,
this agony.   But I cannot at all agree with
you that it would be thus sufficient, provided your faith were as strong as you rep-
resent.   That is a faith, you yourself say,
which passeth understanding ; it is rooted
in emotions and longings ; its promises to
you are copious and priceless.   But I cannot reconcile your trust with your tears,
your heavenly confidence with your very
earthly lamentation. What if this friend
who has just breathed his last had come to
you some day and said: 'I am going into

a beautiful country, where I shall be exquisitely happy and whither you shall one day follow me'? Would you fall on his neck and tremble with suffering? Would you seek to detain him from that delightful sojourn by every means in your power?... Come, now; there is either a grave flaw in your well-jointed, oft-vaunted armor of faith, or you have deceived both yourself and others with regard to its resistance, its durability. For it fails to stand the one needed test. It is impotent in the face of that very calamity which it boasts of underrating. At the door of the tomb it falters and loses courage. If I had it I make bold to say that I would see joy in the dead man's obsequies, and resent as irrelevant the mournful emblem on his door-bell. You are an optimist, yet you have not the due and consistent courage of one when it comes to a question of bearing that very ordeal which you rebuke me for calling crucially severe.... Now, let us see how far this same alleged courage will serve you with relation to the laws of living—those laws, remember, which you name the product of a supreme Benignity, ever watchful for your welfare. How do you really oppose the unpleasant stress of poverty? By ardent prayer? I do not deny that you may pray devoutly, but do you not also take pains to work with industry as well, and to exert all your faculties of unsullied trades-manship toward the end of gaining a com-fortable livelihood? By prayer, too, you may seek to rid yourself of countless other ills ; but if you should to-morrow discover that your cellar was filled with stagnant water, would you not instantly resort to the services of a competent drainer? If an earthquake should suddenly shake your house, would you drop on your knees, or would you rush with expedition from the doorway? If your child fell ill to-day of scarlet-fever, would prayer or medicine be first in your parental thought? And yet you would denounce as unpardonably 'godless' the man who should presume to speak with you of the inefficacy of prayer. The arrogance of optimism would swiftly rise in revolt against his theories. I do not, be it borne in mind, deny the assertiveness of my own pessimism. And yet I seldom get even the chance of exploiting it. The large mass of 'civilization' to which you belong will rarely accord me that chance. You are always crying at me from your pulpits, your church-meetings, your popular assemblages of many sorts. When I point to John Stuart Mill's essay *On Nature* you shudder, and marvel how I can be so 'materialistic.' And yet, practically, you treat Nature as the same implacable foe that I treat her. If a sharp wind rushes from the north, you button your great-coat over your chest. If you read in your sympathizing newspapers that several wretched Italian immigrants have been detained at quarantine, reeking with the microbes of cholera, you have dismal dreams of a horrified Broadway and a demoralized Fifth Avenue. You are, in other words, as much of an active, operative pessimist as I am, and the only positive difference between us is that you orally proclaim an optimism which I will not proclaim at all, since I cannot live up to it, nor take pleasure in flagellating my fellow-creatures with its arrogance— its arrogance, on which I am never tired, in my present arraignment of you, aggrievedly to harp."

There is no doubt that a so-called " healthy" state of the human mind generally, if not always, is allied to one of stupidity. If we think at all of whence we have come, whither we are going, and wherefore we are here, we inevitably recoil from that

trinity of mysteries ; and to let our thoughts
dwell habitually upon any subject invested
with so much gloomy dissatisfaction and
unrest is of course an occupation highly
injurious to happiness. There can be no
doubt, either, that idiots and animals, when
freed from bodily pain, are perfectly happy.
Still, on the other hand, it is not denied
that contentment is incompatible with
brains, for the simple reason that very
many persons are as firm-nerved and as
fearless in their contemplation of *le grand
peut-être* as Napoleon was on the eve of
a battle. But there is no excuse for
beings thus endowed with perennial fortitude to cast scorn upon others of weaker
mould ; for if the manifold ills of life keenly
alarm me and do not disconcert my neighbor, the point as to whether my agitation
or his imperturbability is most in order
must be solely determined by the inimical
degree of the assailant agency ; and only
fools will persist in saying that life is not
pregnant with ills. Wise men may offset
these ills with blessings, but the latter still
remain convertible at even a moment's
notice into their distinct reverse, while
many of the former, such as old age, death,
sundering of attached souls, bereavement,

the failure of eyesight or hearing, are without cure, consolation, alleviation. Nor do
the Latin words, *Pulvis et umbra sumus*,
thoroughly convey the surpassing melancholy of human life. Ours is not merely
a world where we die. It is one in which
heredity exerts an increasing and inexorable mastery. The edicts of heredity,
expressed in Biblical phrase by "the sins of
the fathers . . visited upon the children,"
are too often as tyrannous as any that a
Nero or a Caligula could devise. Our asy-
lums and hospitals make harshly plain to
us the unmerited woes that are visited upon
generations of mortals. There we may see
diseases transmitted by progenitors to their
descendants which entail years of torment
that the worst despot history can produce
would have been loath to visit upon his
guiltless victims. Adults and little children
alike quiver beneath the lash of these deplorable inflictions. Inherited rheumatic
gout will twist and distort the limbs of an
infant from its birth until it has reached
nine or ten years, and then kill it in the end,
ruthlessly and with perhaps only a slight
moribund interval of surcease from excessive pain. Inherited cancer lingeringly
slays both saint and sinner with frigid dis-

regard of either desert or innocence. The
babe is born to live a week, a month, a year,
and then perish with pangs that make us
thankful its racked and persecuted little
body could cease from breathing when it
did. The middle-aged are flung upon beds
of misery by some malady which has been
slowly, insidiously developing within them
while they labored for the peaceful compe-
tence which now at last they have just attained, and no more. The old are stricken
by the same hideous ailment which destroyed their fathers or mothers at a similar
age. (Heredity has, in its demoniac quiver,
arrows tipped with a poison more baneful
than any of which the Borgias ever
dreamed.)

Nor is this all. The optimist may toss
his head as merrily and dissentiently as he
will, but that very "spiritual" part of us
whose divine origin he is so fond of extol-
ling as indestructible, has its throes to endure, for which no merciful anæsthetic has
yet been invented by psychologist or meta-
physician. To love and to be loved in this
life may present ineffable enjoyment. But
to love and to be loved are forever forming
the saddest of *non-sequiturs.* It is not always,
by any means, that the intervention of caste

and wealth tears two lovers apart from one
another. Nature, no less than man, has her
Montague and her Capulet, her Abelard
and her Heloise. A man adores, worships
a certain woman, and finds her cold to him
as marble. A woman is stirred by the same
unquenchable preferment, and is met by
the same stolid indifference. Such passions
as these, thwarted in their very births, are
at once the marvel and the despair of all
whom they besiege. They are like birds
with bleeding and shattered wings ; they
are powerless to fly, and can only crawl
along with their smarting burdens. George
Eliot (whose morality and charity as a
writer are immense, yet whose pessimism
is no less a fact to all who have studied her
faithfully) touches, in "Daniel Deronda,"
on this wide, eternal reality of the lover's
unrequited affection. Women hide it more
than men—and suffer more on this account.
Men have larger means for seeking and
obtaining forgetfulness. Perhaps very few
of either sex fail ultimately to heal their
aching wounds. But when such love as
theirs has become simply memory, the sting
that succeeds its disappearance is sometimes a persistent, if not a poignant one.
How could we ever so vehemently have

loved and yet now feel this torpid callous-
ness in a heart that was once so tremu-
lously sensitive? Our love, when we were
thralled by it, made us feel a sacred kin-
ship with the stars ; we looked into the red
bosoms of roses and the balmy chalices of
lilies, with new eyes for their richness and
chastity; our most prosaic tasks took a
halcyon edge upon their very commonness
and dulness, like ordinary objects when seen
through prisms. We pressed our friends'
hands more warmly than had been our wont,
because friendship was allied with love, and
love was a divine melody that every wind
sang to us, every sunbeam laughed to us.
...But, deserted by all that old, delicious
exaltation, we ask ourselves what its frenzy
could have meant or been? How may we
any longer call it ideal and poetic when it
has passed away from us with no more
ceremony in its quick evanishment than if
it were an impulse of hunger or a prefer-
ence of claret over champagne? Never do
we seem more clearly to ourselves the transient shadows of a void and profitless dream
than then, in such disillusionized and
doubly solitary hours ! Shakespeare, held
by those highest in critical authority as
the greatest poet that mankind has thus

far been called upon to admire, is the
author of many a pessimistic verse. Indeed, it is the belief of that fearless and
wonderful reasoner, Robert G. Ingersoll
(himself a profound Shakespearian scholar),
that the author of "Hamlet" was a confirmed agnostic and freethinker. Opponents
of this theory will eagerly seize upon the
dramatic form of Shakespeare's work as
ample justification of every "impious" line
he ever wrote. But how about the "Sonnets"? Do they not literally overflow with
thought such as this :

" Since sweets and beauties do themselves forsake,
   And die as fast as they see others grow;
   And nothing'gainst Time's scythe can make defence..."

Or again, these meaning verses :

" Devouring Time, blunt thou the lion's paws,
   And make the earth devour her own sweet brood;
   Pluck the keen teeth from the fierce tiger's jaws
   And burn the long-liv'd phœnix in her blood...;
   But I forbid thee *one most heinous crime :*
   O carve not with thy hours my love's fair brow..."

Or again :

" When I consider everything that grows
      Holds in perfection but a little moment,
   That this huge state presenteth naught but shows
      Whereon the stars in secret influence comment..."

Or again :

" Roses have thorns and silver fountains mud;
    Clouds and eclipses stain both moon and sun,
    And loathsome canker lives in sweetest bud..."

Or, still once again :

"Since brass, nor stone, nor earth, nor boundless sea,
    But sad mortality o'ersways their power,
How with this rage shall beauty hold a plea,
    Whose action is no stronger than a flower?"

Or, still once again, and the last time,
though many more similar passages of
gloom and despondency could be cited,
let us now reproduce the whole of a son-
net which has long been famed as one of
the brightest jewels in this very remarkable collection. A more plaintive moan of
despairing revolt against the entire earthly
scheme was never uttered by any poet, living or dead.

" Tired with all these, for restful death I cry,—
    As, to behold desert a beggar born,
    And needy nothing trimm'd in jollity,
    And purest faith unhappily forsworn,
    And gilded honor shamefully misplac'd,
    And maiden virtue rudely strumpeted,
    And right protection wrongfully disgrac'd,
    And strength by limping sway disabled,
    And art made tongue-tied by authority,
    And folly (doctor-like) controlling skill,

And simple truth miscall'd simplicity.
And captive good attending captain ill :
  Tired with all these, from these would I be gone,
  Save that, to die, I leave my love alone."

Such denunciations of life, vented by
Shakespeare, are in the poet's own voice,
and not that of any portrayed dramatic
character. The poet here speaks through
his individual lips, and not those of any
malign creation like Iago or Macbeth.
" This little life is rounded by a sleep," and
" All the world's a stage " are but two, as it
were, among the multitudinous black pearls
of thought which help to make up that
other truly royal chaplet. What would the
modern newspaper say to ideas like these,
if so illustrious an authority had not uttered
them ? Here are some words of condemnation against pessimism, taken a day or two
ago from a New York daily journal of
prominence and power:

"An author who depicts life in dreary
colors is sure to exert a most undesirable
influence over many of his readers. The
force of this applies to all kinds of writing.
Whether a man pens an epic poem or a
newspaper editorial, the tone of his philos·
ophy is sure to leave its ultimate effect on
those who peruse his words. Is it not then

incumbent upon an author to shun, as far
as possible, that mocking pessimism which
in our day serves to cover a vast amount of
mental inability? One word in literature
by an optimistic thinker is worth ten thousand by a grumbler, even though the latter
may adorn his thoughts with the brightest
gems of wit and poesy."

The above is a most salient example of
the arrogance of optimism. This little
group of sentences may be said to contain
the same condescension and patronage
which mark uncounted pages of our current
newspapers. It is always the same *à priori*
course of mingled laudation and damnation
Why is one word of optimism worth ten
thousand of pessimism? If neither manner
of surveying life can be set aside as in-
nately false, why should this be upheld and
applauded while that is decreed to "cover
a vast amount of mental inability"? Do
the sonnets of Shakespeare, that mourn so
eloquently and untiringly "the wreckful
siege of battering days," perpetrate such a
flimsy concealment? Was George Eliot a
"grumbler" because she wrote that heart-
breaking story of "Middlemarch," where
destiny rewards hardly a single noble intent
or disinterested yearning? Did the shrewd

lips of Voltaire lie when they reminded us
that 'we never live, but are always in expectation of living'? If, as Montaigne somewhere axiomates, 'ignorance is the mother
of all evils,' why should it exert ''an undesirable influence'' to depict life in ''dreary
colors,'' when those dreary colors are all
borrowed from the sure shadows cast by
every-day occurrences? Have the stimulating prophecies and warrants of Christianity prevented a million cases of madness,
a million acts of suicide? Allowing all the
beauty, allurement, pastime, lofty pursuit,
glorious intoxication of life to be credible
and tangible, why should its ugliness, re-
pulsion, disappointment, failure, overthrow,
receive but furtive glances, as though fable
had first begotten and fatuity afterward
exaggerated them? Is the optimistic fer-
mentation brought about in unenlightened
minds by sermons like those of Dr. Talmage and others equal to a tranquil facing
of verities—a square and honest confront-
ing of the whole sweet-and-bitter, dark-and-
bright enigma, and a frank subsequent con-
fession that both our laughter and our groans
are the products of an inscrutable, abysmal,
tantalizing source? If I concede your
right to say that the Mediterranean breaks

with voluptuous cadences on the shores of
the Riviera, why should you refuse me my
right to answer that the cyclone is death-
fully raging in the wilds of Nebraska?
But the arrogance of optimism does refuse
me this right. It chides me and frowns
upon me when I maintain that Emerson's
amiable treatise concerning Nature is but
the complement of John Stuart Mill's dolorous one, and that while each may be in
its way undeniable, the first only leaves
off where the last begins. If optimism
could *disprove* the avowals of pessimism it
would be quite another affair with her.
But she cannot ; she can only berate and
abuse them. And yet the professedly buoy-
ant members of society are the very ones
who tell you that they have had " oh, such
a wretched attack of the blues," or that
they have heard Brown's book is doleful,
and therefore do not want to read it, since
*there is such an enormous amount of sadness in
life that one cannot escape,* whether he will or
no. (It is usually the person impartially
observant of life in *all* her phases who has
the best time as years crowd upon him.) The
present article offers no plea for pessimism,
no recommendation of its counsels, no en-
dorsement of its assumptions and prem-

ises. But a plea certainly is offered for the respectful consideration of a doctrine so much of which is irrefutable truth. If it be not too commonplace, I would suggest that the kind of truth we men and women want most of all—the kind to live by and to die by—is midway between these two strenuous extremes. The crown of a perfect education might be defined as a perfect freedom from prejudice. It is extraordinary how much of a peculiar sort of prejudice the optimist of to-day fosters. It would seem as if he were only arrogant with living pessimists, and forgivingly overlooked the sins of all others. We occasionally find him allowing greatness to Voltaire ; he has been known to discredit the story that Thomas Paine died in miseries of repentance, imploring the pardon of heaven for his blasphemies. But not to *faire des examples* with too much prolixity, we note that the optimist abides unruffled in his contemplation of what are perhaps the most daring pessimisms ever put into verse. I mean those of Omar Khayyám, the Persian astronomer-poet. When, about thirty years ago, the late Mr. Edward Fitzgerald rendered these astonishing stanzas into admirable English verse, it was curious

to observe the popularity they at once secured. Both here and in England optimism
was never weary of praising them.   It was
so safe to do so ; Omar had been born seven
hundred years ago ; there was nothing sac-
rilegious in hearing the voice of materialism at that distance away.   And so the optimist would smile to himself as he read of
the old poet's *vie orageuse* and the epicurean
conclusions that he had drawn from it. That
book, to half the optimists in the land, was
like a "jolly bank-holiday " to a lot of London clerks. They interchanged shocked
looks as they read, but with none the less
avidity they *did* read—

> " What, without asking, hither hurried *whence ?*
> And, without asking, *whither* hurried hence ?
> O many a cup of this forbidden wine
> Must drown the memory of that insolence !"

Of course, they argued, if any modern
human being, such as Col. Ingersoll, should
speak in the style of the following quat-
rain, it would be outrageous to the last
degree.   But then it sounded so much less
abominable (it sounded so fascinatingly
quaint, in fact !) when you heard a voice
pealing forth from a seven-hundred-year-
old past with such words as these :

"Oh, Thou, who didst with pitfall and with gin
Beset the road I was to wander in,
Thou wilt not with predestined evil round
Enmesh, and then impute my fall to sin !"

Still, with all the dilettante laxity which
the optimist is known to have permitted
himself regarding the perusal of Omar
Khayyám's Rubáiyát, it is difficult to understand how he could quite have steadied
his nervous system sufficiently for a placid
consideration of the following—perhaps
more scathingly militant against accepted
codes than anything in the whole most un-
conventional poem :

"Oh, Thou, who man of baser earth didst make,
And even with paradise devise the snake,
For all the sin wherewith the face of man
Is blackened, man's forgiveness give—and take!"

I recall that, when Omar Khayyám's little
book was first published in this country, a
certain gentleman who had been one of its
earliest and most enthusiastic readers im-
parted to me his private suspicions concerning its actual authorship : "I feel convinced," he said, "that this 'astronomer-
poet of Persia' is a graceful myth, invented
by the Rev. Edward Fitzgerald himself, in
order to conceal his own athestic tendencies." I could not help thinking this a

rather singular course and plan by which a clergyman should seek to win his *bâton maréchal* as a poet, and subsequent developments proved my friend's hypothesis to have been a mistaken one. But I have often afterward ruminated upon the general social result of a discovery that the Rubáiyát had really been the work of a Chatterton-like literary impostor. Ah, what recantations and retractions would have poured from the lips of our mortified optimists, if they had been called upon to regard all these acrid and sinister sayings as the outcome of a living, breathing pessimist, and not of one that had been romantically and picturesquely dead for seven long centuries ! It is doubtful if Mr. Elihu Vedder would have presumed to make those very imaginative and captivating illustrations of his, which now accompany at least one precious edition of the work, and which, moreover, in all their bitter and often terrible beauty, are treasured by optimists of every sect, from Roman Catholic to Unitarian.

The arrogance of optimism will probably cease to exert itself when it has received from evolution a disclosure of its own hypocrisy. For very few of us can live at

all without being in a measure pessimists. "Theologians have exausted in-
genuity," says Ingersoll, "in finding ex-
cuses for God." But this is not so bold,
after all, as the remark of the Frenchman
who said that the sole excuse for the deity
was "*qu'il n'existe pas.*" Still, whether we
revolt or submit, it is very apt to be one
and the same with us : we are what George
Eliot has somewhere called "yoked crea-
tures with private opinions." None of us
can afford to sneer at him who looks more
sombrely than we do at the unutterable
wretchedness of the world, or at him who
distrusts more thoroughly than ourselves
the sinful and selfish races that people it.
Advancement in knowledge will bring pessimist and optimist nearer together. If
there are any who refuse sunshine its ra-
diance, flowers their bloom and odor, human love its tenderness and majesty, pity
its tears and almsgiving, virtue its cleanli-
ness and candor, justice its righteousness
and nobility,—if there continue any so partisan and feeble of judgment as this, then
optimism may turn didactic to her heart's
content, and with an unassailable authority.
In the meantime let her use against the
"fallacies" of her foe other weapons than

those of idle invective. (Let her imitate the calm methods of science, who condemns nothing, sneers at nothing, but accepts, investigates, analyzes, utilizes all.) You cannot make me think malaria, lightning, earthquake, rattlesnakes, treason, malice, falsehood, meanness are less of the curses I know them, because you cry out at me that I am a malicious fool, and endanger the welfare of life and society by noting too closely such uncanny developments. Neither can I make you think the warble of birds, the murmur of streams, the limpid-ness of heaven, the flocculence and purity of a summer cloud, the exuberance and del-icacy of a rose, the mirth and innocence of childhood, the dignity and strength of hon-est manhood, the rapture of a maiden's first love, the sanctity of a mother's protective caress, are slighter blessings than I know them, because you cry out at me that I am a mawkish sentimentalist, and endanger the welfare of life and society by dwelling with too much emphasis upon these especially agreeable phenomena. Some day, when their present constituents long have been dust, these two inimical factions of intellectuality, optimism and pessimism, will meet on a common ground—that of mutual concession and conciliation. Some day? And yet who shall dare to dream what far grander results that future day may accomplish? Science may then have scaled heights which we now hold insuperable for even *her* dauntless foot. The whole order of seeing and believing may be changed. What now seems to us finality, may then have become the rudimentary commonplace of physics. If the twentieth century marches along at the same superb pace as that of the nineteenth, there is no prophesying—there is hardly any fanciful guessing, even—what invaluable certitudes respecting life, death and the human soul *may* be reached! Nor is there anything millennial, utopian, impracticable in such a deduction. Not so very long ago the mere mention of an era in which instantaneous submarine communication between Europe and America was attainable, would have been scoffed at as the wildest of fanatical visions. It may be that in the twentieth or twenty-first century pessimism and optimism will be so welded together into a wider conception of what is now deemed insoluble that the 'arrogance' which this protest has attempted to exhibit will have grown as inconsiderable an issue as many a present optimist, after reading thus far, will feel disposed to pronounce it.

THE BROWNING CRAZE.

CRITICAL surprise has been more than
once expressed, of late, that in an age so
militant against the development of the
poetic spirit, a single man should find himself (and that, too, at an advanced period
of his life) surrounded, not to say besieged,
by hosts of ardent admirers. Everybody
has now heard of the "Browning Craze,"
and it is quite probable that many had
heard of it while Mr. Robert Browning
himself was hardly more to them than a
meaningless name. And yet to the majority of literary men and women in England
and America this cult has long been a
familiar one. Not until perhaps a decade
ago did it begin to assume its present spacious proportions. I remember meeting
devout Browningites at least twenty years
ago, when almost a boy. And as boys will,
when their thoughts turn toward the letters
of their time and land, I soon felt an ambitious craving to graduate into a Browningite myself.

Such a worship then possessed so fascinating an element of rarity ! It was so at-
tractive a rôle for one to give a compas-
sionate lifting of the brows and say, " No,
really ?" when somebody declared himself
quite unable to understand the obscure
author of " Sordello." You knew perfectly
well that any number of his lines were
Hindostanee to you, and yet you made use
of your patronizing pity and your " No,
really ?" all the same. There is safety in the
assertion that Mr. Browning has driven more
pedantic youngsters to unblushing falsehood than any other writer in the language.
All sorts of roads lead to fame, and his,
oddly indeed, has been the very oblique one
of an unpopularity which bore superficial
signs that it was preferred and courted.
But a deeper glance assures the unbiassed
observer that this is by no means fact. Almost every poem of the many which he has
written bears evidence that the attitudina-
rian has been at work, that the conscious
trickster has again and again superseded the
conscientious artist, and that the notoriety
we too often give caprice and whimsicality
has been aimed after with a studied zeal.
It is in this way that Mr. Browning inces-
santly betrays what might be called the

frivolity inseparable from his temperament. Take, for example, in "Men and Women," his most coherent collection of dramatic and lyrical poetry, the profusion of rank affectations mingled with their hardy opposites. Indeed, this one book, which is by far the most serene, lucid and endurable that he has ever given to the world, contains much that art cannot fail to find hideous, even repulsive. Scarcely a poem is exempt from some shocking flaw. In "A Lover's Quarrel," which possesses good human touches, if the verse does jerk like a sled on a road filmed meagrely with snow, we read such rhymed crudity as

> See the eye, by a fly's foot blurred—
> Ear, when a straw is heard
> Scratch the brain's coat of curd !

But effects of unpardonable bathos like this abound in "Men and Women." The present essay would exceed all allowable scope if half of them were quoted. Poems which have received rapturous praise fairly teem with them. In "The Statue and the Bust" (a piece of work so often declared faultless) there are obscurities of construction for which a school-boy would be rated by his teacher. "Master Hugues of Saxe-

Gotha" racks and tortures the most ordinary ear. "Childe Roland to the Dark Tower Came" (another object of devout veneration) has little about it that is metrically slipshod, but affects an impartial reader, after finishing it, as a lyric literally torn from an unwilling talent; its very rhymes have a forced, factitious queerness, and its abrupt ending seems to exclaim, "Look at my wonderful suggestiveness of allegory!" And we look, if our eyes are not bloodshot with the "Browning Craze," only to conclude that the entire poem is on such mystical stilts as to transcend the reach of all sensible interpretation. "Popularity," which endeavors to laud the superiority of genius over mere facile aptitude, ends with two stanzas regarding "Hobbs, Nobbs, Stokes, and Nokes," which few living men of taste would have cared to print at all, and none except their creator would have cared to offer his public as poetry. "Old Pictures in Florence" repeatedly massacres what should be a mellifluous anapæstic measure, and leaves you as tired of its eccentric attitudinizing as if you had been button-holed by some loquacious rhapsodist in one of the Arno-fronting streets.

But it would be idle, on the other hand, to deny "Men and Women" both poems and passages of poems glowing with merit. We find there "Evelyn Hope," a bit of passion worth careful heed, though overrated by its lovers because so massively self-satisfied in its transcendentalism. We find "Bishop Blougram's Apology," a brilliant study of a narrow, glib, specious-tongued prelate, and interesting if on no other ground than its dramatic exposition of a meretricious moralist. We find the tender and pathetic "Andrea del Sarto," whose sole objection is the mannered and inharmonious blank verse which Mr. Browning always employs. We find the fervid little "Love among the Ruins," and wish its author, so often insolent in his defiance of art, had chosen to sing many more times like that for the delight of folk unborn. We find "Saul," burning with eloquence and yet perfectly intelligible, notwithstanding its cloying pietism. We find "In a Balcony," perhaps the best piece of drama Mr. Browning has ever written. We find "The Last Ride Together," an ardent episode of love-making, but lyrically spoiled by its far-fetched subtleties of simile and illustration. We find "Any Wife to Any

Husband," which to read over ten times
very patiently and studiously is to convince us that it is fine—and what more of
critical irony could be heaped on a poem
than that? We find "Two in the Cam-
pagna," which begins exquisitely and gets
labored and befogged toward the end. We
find "A Grammarian's Funeral," which
makes the blood beat quicker, in parts, and
in parts lamentably cools it. We find "A
Toccata of Galuppi's," which gives us a
laugh or two as excellent Italian comedy.
And lastly we find "Fra Lippo Lippi,"
winsome, sweet, and a poem which Tennyson might have told to us in verse as en-
chanting as that in which he has embalmed
" Tithonus."

It has been the writer's deliberate purpose
to deal first with "Men and Women," for
this book, in its entirety, faults and virtues
both included, will most probably mark the
uncrumbling corner-stone of Mr. Browning's future fame. Before this he had written a very sane and splendid poem called
"How they Brought the Good News from
Ghent to Aix." It is so fine a piece of
work, indeed, that I can easily imagine his
worshippers despising it. It is no nut to
crack; it shows what an artist its parent

might have been. Published originally in the same volume, if I mistake not, was " My Last Duchess," a brief enough thing, which has attained an extraordinary reputation for no apparent cause. It has the *chute de phrase* of a cruel' man speaking heartlessly about a wife whom his neglect killed. But, except for the mild shudder it awakens, it is in no sense noteworthy, and the verse drags and hobbles with so much sluggishness that no one save the " professional reader" (a great friend of Mr. Browning's, because elocution helps the latter's frequent disjointed and staccato technics) can ever succeed in rendering it rightly. Among the earlier " Dramatic Lyrics" must be remembered " The Pied Piper of Hamelin," one of the few English poems that have achieved a deserving popularity among the masses. It is a child's poem, and therefore its occasional *bizarre* falsetto may be pardoned. Not so " The Flight of the Duchess," however, in which a charming and most spiritual tale is told somewhat after the style of an Ingoldsby Legend or Bab Ballad. It is filled with such rhymes as " tintacks" and " syntax," " stir-up" and " syrup," " news of her," and " Lucifer," and many others equally un-

suited to a history at once so serious and
so exalted. Here we are confronted with
that deliberated oddity which might be
termed Mr. Browning's most irritating
fault, as it certainly is his least honest one.
We see that he has planned all these fire·
cracker surprises of diction ; they bear
slight resemblance to that "rough power"
by which his artistic laziness has so often
been misnamed. For there is a certain
class of critics (and, I regret to add, a large
one) who only need the evidence of an
author's bad rhymes, haphazard rhythms
and defective constructions in order to discover that he fairly bristles with " rough
power." *Le mot juste*, the polished and accurate utterance, is in severe disrepute
with these persons. It has been they who
for years have flung their jibes at the
unrivalled perfection of Lord Tennyson's
verse. Apparently, as they love to put it,
the latter had not power because it was
not " rough." He was mincing because
he never slurred a line ; he lacked the
higher kind of emotion because he had
patiently chiselled his work into a dignity
above the frenzies of Byron or the hysteria
of Shelley. I sometimes wonder, for my
own part, if those cavillers who ring such

wearisome changes on this one theme have ever considered how much great power is often at the root of poetical grace. Even if Tennyson were only felicitous (and he is that besides being a very noble poet as well) he would have accomplished much. All the remarkable poets who ever lived have had as much grace as grandeur. Grace is frequently inseparable from grandeur, but when it is not it is never weakness; it is always strength. The elastic step and flexible form of some delicate maiden may typify an endurance and fortitude not possessed by the sturdiest athlete.

Just as there were thousands of people who would have lost all regard for Carlyle if he had been dowered with a decorous and not an uncouth English idiom, so there are thousands to-day who would consider Mr. Browning's poetry very tame indeed were it not studded with such points of ugliness and idiosyncrasy as those which disfigure "The Flight of the Duchess." But other poems that belong to Mr. Browning's earlier manner, that were published among the two or three collections with which, years ago, he first presented the world, and that deserve deep if not unqualified commendation, are "Soliloquy in a Spanish Cloister," "The Confessional," and "Holy-Cross Day." All these are alive with vigor, and not always by any means impossible to understand after a second or third reading—which is saying a good deal against them, perhaps, in the opinion of the confirmed Browningite. "Holy-Cross Day" is an especially original and striking presentation of the Jew's degraded condition during the Middle Ages. Nothing can be more trenchant than its incidental sarcasms, nothing more acute than the reproaches it hurls against the bigotries and hypocrisies of its time.

All these better and wiser poems of Mr. Browning appeared many years ago. "Sordello" had, unless I err, preceded them, and from the absurd enigma of that book their comparative clearness was a welcome change. Mr. Browning began to be hailed as a poet emergent from darkness, and in a few quarters bright hopes were entertained of his future. "Sordello," when heeded at all, may have made the cynics jest and the thoughtful look grieved, but we have no record that it had more materially injured the young versifier who had chosen to masquerade in it *en sphinx*. Everybody knows the story of how Barry Cornwall's

wife gave him the book during his con-
valescence after a great illness, and of how
he read the first page bewilderedly, then
amazedly, and at length in nervous terror.
Handing it a little later to his wife, he
asked the tremulous question, "What do
you make of this?" And when, some fif-
teen or twenty minutes afterwards, Mrs.
Proctor replied, "I don't understand a
word of it," her husband burst forth in
delight,. "*Thank God I am not mad!*" This
tale may or may not be false, but it certainly bears the stamp of probability. I recall, in about my eighteenth year, discred-
iting the statements I had heard relative to
"Sordello's" unintelligibility, and attempt-
ing to read the book with a confidence in
my own anti-Philistine comprehension of
it. But a few pages convinced me that
report had not falsified its odious "tough-.
ness." Beautiful gleams occur in it, but
they are like flying lights over a surface of
heavy darkness. Now and then, for twenty
lines or so, you feel as if you had smoothly
mastered its meaning; again, all is dis-
array and density. It is like seeing a fine
statue reflected in a cracked mirror: here
is the curve of a symmetric arm, but you
follow it only to meet an abortive bulge of

elbow ; there is the outline of a sculptur-
esque cheek, but you trace below it a repellent deformity of throat ; once more
you light with joy upon a thigh of faultless moulding, but lower down you are
shocked by obese distortion. The whole
"poem" resembles a caricature of some
Gothic cathedral, in planning which some
demented architect has treated his own
madness to a riot of gargoyles. The *en-
semble* is monstrous, inexcusable. But, like
many of Mr. Browning's later modern
poems, it strikes you as more of a wilful
failure than a feeble one.

All the plays of this author were published by him while he was still a young
man. He calls himself, in one of his lyrics,
"Robert Browning, you writer of plays,"
and it is evident, from the dramatic spirit
informing a great deal of his verse, that he
believed himself with extreme seriousness
to be a dramatist of high rank. Eulogy
untold has been poured upon him in this
capacity. Long before the "Browning
Craze" had developed its first febrile symp-
toms, no less an authority than Dickens
was reported to have exclaimed, in a burst
of enthusiastic reverence, that he would
rather have written "A Blot in the 'Scut-

cheon " than all the novels to which his
name was signed ! It seems impossible
that the creator of "David Copperfield "
could ever have made any such wantonly
random declaration. And yet, not very
long ago, an English writer of some distinction endeavored to prove that " Strafford,"
" Colombe's Birthday," and " The Return
of the Druses" had been successfully performed before London audiences. They
may have been performed, but that they
were in any degree successful cannot for
an instant be credited. They are not
dramas at all ; they are no more than dia-
logues divided arbitrarily into acts. And
yet they have been compared to the plays
of Shakespeare by several inflammable
zealots in the Browning cause. Still, after
all, writers have existed who rejoiced, during the past two hundred years, in heaping
odium upon Shakespeare as a charlatan,
and we all recollect the contempt with which
Sir Samuel Pepys wrote of him, not to mention Oliver Goldsmith's freely-expressed
disdain in the " Vicar of Wakefield." Thus
it becomes apparent that human taste has
many foibles and vagaries, and that the
blare of a few partisan trumpets cannot do
much for the establishment of·a genuine

literary fame. As for that mightily be-
lauded play, "A Blot in the 'Scutcheon,"
it was accorded an admirable oral chance
at the Star Theatre in New York, two or
three years ago. Mr. Lawrence Barrett
took the part of Tresham, and all the other
characters, as the newspapers put it, were
"in good hands." Mr. Barrett and all his
company did their best for the play. At
the end of the third act I heard somebody
near me murmur that it was "Oh, im-
mensely fine, don't you know, but a closet-
play . . . yes, decidedly a closet-play." I
could not help asking myself whether the
reputation which it had through years enjoyed were not a sort of closet-reputation
as well. For my own part, I had heard it
somewhat apathetically and mechanically
called "marvellous" and "grand" a great
many times, before I attempted to read it,
by people who used these epithets as though
they were somehow pledged to propriety
for their correct delivery. But I realize
now that it is a work of talented adroitness
and little more. There is something curiously professorial and factitious about it,
brought forth more clearly by the foot-
lights than by perusal, and yet perceptible
through either medium. Its "psychology"

becomes overburdening, oppressive. Everybody, from the first scene till the last, is on transcendental stilts ; nor is such impression diminished by the blunt, choppy character of Mr. Browning's blank verse. As Tresham is made to fling this forth in sentence after sentence, his character grows more and more unsympathetic. He is meant to be the ideal of honor and nobility, and he gradually becomes to us, during the progress of the piece, more and more of a petulant metaphysician. He says to the seducer of his sister, on finding him at the casement of this lady, about to enter it surreptitiously at night,-

> "We should join hands in frantic sympathy
> If you once taught me the unteachable,
> Explained how you can live so, and so lie.
> With God's help I retain, despite my sense,
> The old belief—a life like yours is still
> Impossible.   Now draw."

Could the far-fetched be carried much further than to make a bluff English cavalier talk (and especially under these conditions of anguish and preoccupation) in a strain of such hair-splitting highfalutinism ? As for the killing of Mertoun by Tresham, it becomes, considering his approaching marriage to Mildred, almost ridiculous as a tragic expedient. We cannot but feel how much safer than a *femme couverte* that sister, married to her imprudent boyish lover, would have remained for the rest of her life. And regarding the way in which Mildred not merely forgives but *blesses* the slayer of him whom she worshipped, I will venture to affirm that there was not a single auditor in the Star Theatre on the night of the performance to which I have alluded, who did not feel that here a note of the very falsest exaggeration had been struck. But the " Browning Craze" was in full fury at that time, and perhaps not a few qualms of natural dislike were loyally repressed. Of the many incontestable merits that belong to "A Blot in the 'Scutcheon" I will not speak : for a quarter of a century the world has had these dinned into its ears, and alike the friends and foes of Mr. Browning should by this time be well acquainted with them. They are not, in my own judgment, at all equal to the praise with which they have been so lavishly greeted. The play is at best three acts of inexorable grimness, lit by not one ray of humor. To have compared it with any of Shakespeare's masterpieces was by no means a friendly office to perform toward it, since time is apt to avenge such mistakes rather harshly. Perhaps the retribution may be quite tardy in coming : it usually is. *La vengeance est un plat qui se mange froid.* But in the end it is apt to come. No amount of thrifty bushes may reconcile the daintier palate to inferior wine, though when it is good it may need no bush at all.

"Pippa Passes" deserves mention as the most charming of its writer's plays ; but, with the exception of "Paracelsus" (a very voluminous affair, full of untold tedium), it is perhaps the least "actable" of them all. It is, however, a most delightful production, and the only member of its group, I should say, which has not been rated far above its deserts. The others attempt to be plays and are not ; they drag ; they are over-subtle ; they lack freshness or attractiveness of story. But "Pippa Passes," an airy, graceful, and yet deeply significant composition, succeeds, somehow, in being a play without the slightest apparent effort. That it will not act is nothing derogatory to it, for the same view could sensibly be held of " The Tempest."

With these more youthful achievements it might be said that the fame of Mr. Browning passed through its primary

phase. His name, between twenty and
thirty years ago, was rarely spoken without
an accent of mingled admiration and amusement. Few except silly adulators failed
to admit his grave and glaring faults ; few
except those whom such faults drove back
from an acquaintance with him, failed to
perceive that he was dowered with extraordinary natural gifts. By such a poem
as "In a Gondola" he had won his right
to the highest future recognition. "In
a Gondola" was marred by follies of
conception and execution, but it seemed
to foretell a great deal, and it was a dramatic lyric that now and then pierced and
enraptured its reader. Much of it was
superb, and other portions were almost
puerile in their fantastic heedlessness of
performance. There was, up to this point,
no doubt that Mr. Browning could sing
with a new voice, but at the same time a
voice clogged by discordant notes. Would
he ever rid himself of those notes through
a careful study of what art really meant ?
Would he cast aside all his semi-barbarous
peculiarities and rise divested of their en-
cumbering mannerisms?

"The Ring and the Book" proved otherwise. Mr. Browning, with an immense

challenge, flung scorn in the face of those who had hoped the brightest things for his poetic future.

At the time "The Ring and the Book" appeared, Tennyson had set the spire upon his cathedral of majestic song. He had written 'Maud," and its novelty of melody had enchanted thousands ; he had written "The Princess," and its prismatic yet potent verses were known and loved countless miles past the rainy little isle in which he had conceived them ; he had made "In Memoriam" break like a sea upon a thousand shores of thought, throb amid countless caves of speculation and yearning, sob amid unnumbered reaches of passion and regret. Tennyson's fame had already based itself upon undying pediments. Mr. Browning was expected by a few earnest adherents to surpass the Laureate. Another effort came from him, and as "The Ring and the Book" this effort was promptly *obsédé* with flattering bravos.

But what, after all, was it, this "Ring and the Book"? I recall spending a whole summer in trying to make myself believe that it was a great poem. I was then about three-and-twenty years old, and many reviews had counselled me into crediting that

it was something worthy to be put side-and-
side with Milton, Dante and Heaven knows
whom else in the way of epic splendor. I
am tempted to write now with the boyish
animus that filled me then, but in doing so
I must first record that I respected the reviewers very fervently and wanted to prove
I was their mate in funds of devout appreciation. And how I did struggle to bring
about this result! How I beat back the
promptings of my better judgment! How I
insisted upon assuring myself that such
and such a line was not brutally obscure!
How I strove to convince myself that the
telling of the same story over and over
again, even though different mouths thus
told it, was not a travesty upon analytic
poignancy! I was in that servile mood
toward the newspaper critics then, which
may in a measure account for my persistent distrust during later years. . . . And at
last my good angel informed me, toward
autumn, that I had wasted my summer,
that language was never given us to conceal our thought, and that every artist must
either seek to strengthen his expression
through the clarification of it or be content
to have oblivion punish him for such neglect.

"The Ring and the Book" was *le commencement de la fin* with Mr. Browning. It must have made him somewhat like the hero in his own praiseworthy poem, "A Lost Leader," and cost him many rational devotees. But it gained him others. His final poetic step had been taken. He was going to yield himself to freaks and whims; he intended to despise the artist and cultivate the *poseur*.

He has cultivated the *poseur*, nearly always, ever since.

I do not deny the brilliancy of his mistake in writing "The Ring and the Book." To refuse force to that work would be like refusing force to a cyclone. But a cyclone is not a poem. Perhaps nothing so daringly prolix has ever been perpetrated in the whole range of English literature. Hidden away amid the quartz-like Browningese of text lies many a diamond of thought and song. But reading and mining are two different occupations. One cannot well conceive of "The Ring and the Book" dying. Death will will probably not be its fate, but a protracted oblivion will find it instead. Fashion makes people read it and talk about it now, but fashion is often another name for forgetfulness. Human patience will not endure its endless repetitions of the same theme, its terribly tiresome presentations of one bloody and unsavory tale at different angles of vision. You can scarcely see in the whole massive bulk and plan of this metrical monstrosity any trace of the humor which Mr. Browning has occasionally shown elsewhere ; a keener humorous sense would, I think, have saved him from the attempt to saddle poor posterity with so cumbrous a burden. Nor is Mr. Browning's blank verse, even when most clear of meaning, an agreeable species of invention. It is original enough ; its earmarks are not to be confounded with those of any other poet ; but when least marred by parentheses, inversions, involutions, *quos egos* and ellipses, it. is almost never free from a particular trick or conceit, which grows, after incessant recurrence, as much a monotony as an aggravation. This consists in making one substantive stand for several verbs, each verb being at the root, so to speak, of a new and distinct sentence, but all sentences being huddled together in a way that sometimes renders turbid the simplest thought. Let us try to find an instance or two of this painful peculiarity. Take the following, for example, from "The Ring and the Book :"

> "The Canon Caponsacchi, then, was sent
> To change his garb, retrim his tonsure, tie
> The clerkly silk round every plait correct,
> Make the impressive entry on his place
> Of relegation. . ."

Or this, from a like source :

> "What if he gained thus much,
> Wrung out this sweet drop from the bitter Past,
> Bore off this rose-bud from the prickly brake
> To justify such torn clothes and scratched hands,
> And, after all, brought something back from Rome?"

But the illustrations of this most infelicitous tendency could be made to cover pages. And we are now accepting Mr. Browning's blank verse at its best, not at its worst. Its worst is sometimes positively horrifying. Surely the man should have a very wondrous message for humanity who aims to deliver this message as a poet and yet continually scorns to do so as an artist. But, after all, who of us has a hard enough conscience to grant that the artist and the poet are ever separable? Whatever his mentality, his reach of spiritual vision, his command of pungent and illuminative epithet, how shall a writer

presume to disdain form in searching after
the expression of truth ? *Quand on se bat
on ne choisit pas ses armes* may reasonably
explain the method of some hot contestant
against a political or social wrong. But
when the poet fights what he believes to
be worst error, are we not justified in ex-
pecting from him a well-burnished blade
and a wrist whose turns reveal both dexterity and harmonious movement ? To the
merest beginner in verse-making it is com-
monly understood that clashes of conso-
nants are the sorriest destruction of melody.
He must avoid them if he wishes to write
presentable or reputable iambs. And yet
Mr. Browning outrages taste in the following lines, taken at random from his works,
where remain innumerable other specimens,
just as dissonant, strident, and sibilant :

It strikes a Fourth, a Fifth thrusts in its nose . . .
Two must discept . . . has distinguished . . .
God's gold just shining its last where that lodges . . .
Billets that blaze substantial and slow . . .
The Knights who to the Dark Tower's search
    addressed . . .
Fear which stings ease . . .
" You are sick, that's sure," they say . . .
Who breasted, beat Barbarians, stemmed **Persia**
    rolling on . . .
To a city bears a fall'n host's woes . . .

Wagner, Dvorak, Liszt . . . to where . . . trumpets,
    shawms . . .
Adjudges such . . . how canst thou . . . this wise
    bound . . .

And finally, from " Ferishtah's Fancies:"

When my *lips just touched* your cheek . . .

The italics here are my own ; for although
the consonantal gruffness in this last quoted
line is not so striking as that of many
which have preceded it, the contrast between its tender sentiment and its coarsely
unmelodic versification affects one like a
vulgar slap in the face. Multitudes of
other similar lines exist throughout Mr.
Browning's copious work. And I cannot
see how any vigor of idea can excuse such
feebleness of presentation. Surely nature
and life, which are so akin to art, do not
demand of us an indulgence for such un-
happy imperfection. Because a gnarled
and blasted tree bears a few sprays of fresh
and glossy leaves we do not gaze upon it
to the neglect of healthful surrounding
growths. Because we know that a child
or a woman possesses mental charms we
do not tolerate a waspish acerbity of phrase
in either. But from art we exact the near-
est approach to perfection, not the most

zigzag deviation from it. Poetic fame has
no pathway to its temple like that traditional
one to a forlorner goal ; it is not paved with
good intentions ; we insist, indeed, upon
its being quarried from the very marbles
of Pentelicus.

Mr. Browning's published writing since
" The Ring and the Book " need not be
dwelt upon in this essay. Those loyal mani-
acs to the " Browning Craze " have their own
Bedlamite reasons, no doubt, for admiring
"Red Cotton Night-Cap Country " and
" The Inn Album." And, after all, what
(in America, at least) does the " Browning
Craze " signify ? The spirit of American
culture has always been an imitative one,
and not seldom to a snobbish degree. It
was quite in the order of things that the
" Browning Craze " should rise in London,
flow a westerly course, and empty into
Chicago. But it submerged Boston on its
way—or at least partially so. I have no
doubt that in both cities the societies which
have been its offspring possess many intelligent and sincere members. But it is very
improbable that all these members are
either intelligent or sincere. One might
confidently assert that a great many of
them are clouded by dulness and tinctured

with toadyism. It does not require much brains for anybody to perceive that the assumption of a certain taste will produce the appearance of exclusiveness on the part of such an assumer. The jargon of the art-schools, for example, is easily caught, and at almost any exhibition of foreign paintings you will discover that some picture which the general public would turn from as unpardonably quaint, rococo, or audacious will attract a little *côterie* of fervid adorers. Perhaps a few of these may honestly believe that the painter in question is a towering genius ; but the majority are yearning to anoint his locks with spikenard and myrrh solely because he is considered " caviare to the general," above the vulgar herd *et id genus omne.* It is doubtful whether the Browning societies of England have gained as many recruits from any other cliques or associations as from those whom Mr. Gilbert has so mercilessly satirized as the Æsthetes. But to be an æsthete is by no means to be a fool. These persons laugh among each other at the caricatures into which they turn themselves, very much as we may believe that any two augurs did of old. Possibly the Browningites laugh now and then among each

other at the solemn importance with which
they are supposed to inform the digging
out of a poor tortured thought from beneath crushing layers of words. - And when
they reflect at all seriously upon their
undertakings and their achievements, the
result certainly cannot be very edifying.
To become a Browningite is indeed not
to have distinguished one's self for much
sense, either common or uncommon. Hero-
worship is always an unwholesome occupation, even if the hero shine with a truly
glorious light. Yet in the case of Mr.
Browning there is no glorious light at all,
but one put under a bushel, and put there
with not a little of the same insufferable
vanity that made Diogenes take up his
abode in a tub. There are very few broad-
minded and unaffected people who have
read Mr. Browning's poetry, or the worthier
portion of it, who would not be willing
unhesitatingly to tell us that he might have
grown a poet of wide and persistent fame.
But he has chosen so to mantle himself in
the most rash and headlong moods of obscurity, he has so trivialized, cheapened and
frittered away the talents which might
have made him serve efficiently the magnificent art he professes to revere, that his

laurels will turn dry and brittle long before another century has dealt with his present renown. Meanwhile he has a kind of adulation to-day, but one with which no true artist should be content. Indeed, the author of " Fifine at the Fair " and " Pacchiarotto " is no longer an artist, though he who wrote " Pippa Passes " and " Love among the Ruins " may once have closely approximated to such a distinction. He may not be aware of the biting and discreditable fact, but hundreds of those who now " study " and " cultivate " him are beings of the kind who would rave hysterically over some headless and armless torso, if thoroughly sure that the *leve vulgus* would not presume to join in their pedantic chorus, after so forlorn a fragment of sculpture had been excavated and set up for popular inspection.

That Mr. Browning is a poet representative of the age in which he now so eminently flourishes cannot with any fairness be conceded. His work makes one point plain, though it leaves so many others in darkness. The impetus of rationalistic thought seems hardly to have touched him. He is an orthodox believer of the most acquiescent type, as his " Christmas Eve and Easter

Day " would conclusively reveal, apart from
hundreds of other evidences throughout
the vast volume of his work. The sinewy
scientific push of his time has. left him
conservatively unaffected. He regards the
priceless teachings of such men as Herbert
Spencer, Buckle, Tyndall, Huxley and
Lecky with as much unconcern as if he
were a clergyman sanctified by the most
rigid Church-of-England orders. No qualm
of doubt regarding the Thirty-Nine Articles
appears ever to disturb him. He is just as
pious as he is frequently opaque. He refers
to God with that familiarity of personal
acquaintanceship which might distinguish
our own Dr. Talmage. He is perfectly
sure and satisfied on the question not only
of an anthropomorphic deity but on that of
a future immortality, accountability, pardon and punishment. A good deal of
his vagueness is like that of the current
theological treatise ; to the consistent and
logical agnostic of our time it means nearly
the same thing. Those who want their
modern poets to be men permeated by the
so-called materialism of the century will
not find a poet after their own heart in a
singer to whom the divinity of Christ is
romantically indisputable. For some minds

it will seem difficult to accept this kind of poet as great, at an epoch when English philosophy has drawn so sharp a limit before the abyss of the unknowable. Mr. Browning might be inclined to shift the entire burden of ecclesiastic responsibility off his shoulders by declaring that he does not speak for himself but for his countless dramatic characters ; and yet he speaks through no lips except his own when he says, with hardy dogmatism :

> God's work, be sure,
> No more spreads wasted than falls scant !
> He filled, did not exceed, man's want
> Of beauty in this life.

And again :

> ——So hapt
> My chance. HE stood there. Like the smoke
> Pillared o'er Sodom when day broke,—
> I saw Him. One magnific pall
> Mantled in massive fold and fall
> His dread, and coiled in snaky swathes
> About his feet : night's black, that bathes
> All else, broke, grizzled with despair,
> Against the soul of blackness there.
> A gesture told the mood within—
> That wrapped right hand which based the chin,
> That intense meditation fixed
> On his procedure,—pity mixed

With the fulfilment of decree.
Motionless, thus, he spoke to me,
Who fell before his feet, a mass,
No man now.

Bugabooism could not go much further
than this. There is something Calvinistic
in these words, emanent soon afterward
from the mouth of a palpable and tangible
deity :

In the roll
Of judgment which convinced mankind
Of sin, stood many, bold and blind,
Terror must burn the truth into. . . .

These and like passages indicate unmis-
takably that Mr. Browning accepts Christianity in not a few of its most conventional
forms. This may be all well enough ; it is
quite the gentleman's own business if he
goes regularly to church every Sunday and
hears a sermon less involved as to meaning
than one of his own poems and at times
considerably more grammatical. But it
would be idle to claim that he who exhibits
this theologic passivity, this religious com-
plaisance, can be said to rank at all abreast
of his period as a strenuous and catholic
thinker. It is true that the most amaz-
ing doctrines exist with regard to the
right province of poetry and the fitting

equipments of poets, and a multitude of critics, otherwise quite credible, will tell you that it is not half so necessary for the poet to think as to feel. But thinking and feeling, as modern science explains, are pretty nearly one and the same ·thing. Wordsworthian "inspiration" is not esteemed so highly as it was forty years ago. The canons and requisitions of art, however, remain unaltered. Emotion is still a splendidly reputable factor in all poetry when governed by that self-control which is the secret equally of Shakespeare's best verse as it is of Longfellow's or Lord Tennyson's. License of expression has been so often and imprudently praised in poets that an unfortunate abuse of latitude has become far too manifest among English-speaking circles of them. Who has not heard the contemptuous declaration that "there is more truth than poetry" in such and such a statement? If scientific investigation is the reigning intellectual stimulus of our nineteenth century, that is very far from being a cause why poetry should perish. For poetry, we now perceive, is not to be defined as Milton (a great poet) defined it, or as Poe (a very poor one) also defined it. Poetry is life, as all literature is life. But it is life in this different way from the rest of literature, that over it is flung the influence of beauty, and so the phases of human experience are made in turn sublimely, tenderly, or pathetically noteworthy. This influence is like a transfiguring light ; it is presentment, treatment, in a certain limited meaning, enchantment. The subject itself may be more or less susceptible of elevation. Byron had merely to let this light play over such a subject as Venice, Lake Leman, Petrarch's tomb, the stars of heaven, or a storm in the Jura Alps, and enthralling poetic pictures glowed with vividness before the mind. But Burns, as his admirers assert, made a mouse immortal by precisely the same means. Often you hear it affirmed that this or that subject cannot be dealt with by poetry, that it is too mean, too inferior, too recondite, too coarse, too prosaic. In these cases the transfiguring light has been more difficult to throw, or perhaps the imaginative flame and lenses whence it has taken origin have been ill-fed and ill-managed. The more un-ideal the subject the harder to idealize it, to turn it into poetry. And yet we have seen Shakespeare in his creation of " Caliban," Milton

in his "Satan," Coleridge in his "Ancient
Mariner," and Lord Tennyson in his "Vision of Sin," envelop the uncanny and repulsive with a raiment as of magical tissue.
Students of French poetry will remember
"*La Charogne*" of Baudelaire, a poem which
has always struck me with the same effect
as if it were a moonlit dung-heap. I do
not applaud, or even suggest an approval of,
such poetry. But if the dung-heap is there,
so, somehow, is the moonlight; and who
that has read this thrilling poem can forget the melody and eloquence of its last
stanza ?—

> *Alors, O ma beauté, dites à la vermine*
> *Qui te mangera de baisers,*
> *Que je garde la forme et l'essence divine*
> *De mes amours décomposés !*

The English have, as Mr. Browning's
own famous wife said of them, in her
"Aurora Leigh,"

> A scornful insular way
> Of calling the French light.

But, notwithstanding this alleged Gallic
lightness, I do not believe it would be possible for a "Sordello," an "Inn Album," a
"Red Cotton Night-Cap Country," or
even a "Ring and the Book," to have ap-

peared in French without promptly being crushed by the heaviest judicial censure. And what rigid, healthy, uncompromising lessons would Mr. Browning have been taught if he had been born a Frenchman! Not that he could not have learned excellent lessons while still remaining an Englishman. But as a writer of French verse his crimes against style would have suffered condign and relentless punishment. The French would either have long ago made it impossible for him to attain the least celebrity, writing as he has written, or they would have trained and taught him by the simple yet forcible formula, that no great poet can ever achieve greatness through the wilful wrapping up of his meaning. And this is the sin which Mr. Browning has repeatedly, unrepentingly committed. The "craze" which he has succeeded in rousing is one of those inexplicable drifts of literary fashion that mark, both here and in England, our strange passing century. But in England it is not their first similar mistake. They crowned and then discrowned poor Sidney Dobell; they raved over and then flouted Alexander Smith; they lifted Gerald Massey upon a lyric pedestal only to hurl him

downward a little later. For us Ameri-
cans to catch this curious fever is far less
excusable, and a good deal of fatuous,
cringing Anglomania is at the bottom of
it. To-day we are devoutly imitating
British perversity in our genuflection before a very ordinary Russian novelist
named Tolstoï, and both writing and
speaking of that sketchy, padded, interminable tale, "Anna Karénina," as if it
were really a classic masterpiece. But the
gods, as everybody knows, are very angry at
the idea of an International Copyright, and
in their animosity they seem to have made
the American reader their diligent abet-
tor. Until the American reader pays less
attention to the curiosities of transatlantic
literature and more to the honest efforts
enshrined within his own, we cannot hope
for much chance of his even desiring that
Congress shall do her work of reparation
and atonement. He might not, after all,
find it so very unpalatable to exchange his
"Browning Craze" for an Emerson one.
Emerson was a great deal more spiritual
poet than is Mr. Browning, and yet quite
as virile. He had the faculty, also, of con-
veying his thoughts neither in spasms nor
mysticisms. Moreover, he is a wonder-

fully stimulating writer to other minds, and debates and discussions that took either his prose or verse as their text might perhaps bring just as much-profit as wading through pages that too often seem but a turbulent brawl and snarl of verbiage.

One of the most distressing features about Mr. Browning's existent reputation —distressing, I mean, to those who discern and measure its basis of humbug—is the way in which his admirers are never tired of saying that it wholly outshines the renown of Lord Tennyson, and that its possessor has touched, thus far in our century, the high-tide mark of English poetry. So, until not very long since, fanatics cried that Carlyle, with his barbarisms, loomed above that most masterly and dignified of writers, Macaulay ; but now the brief prejudice of the hour has passed, and the morrows have begun to dole out equity, as they generally do, with no matter how tardy a service.

Never was a greater literary injustice perpetrated than the placing of Mr. Browning above Lord Tennyson. The Laureate has indeed served his art with a profound and lovely fidelity, while it is no

exaggeration to state of Mr. Browning
that he has not seldom insulted his as
though it were a pickpocket. "In a Gondola" may be a fine love-lyric; but who
would compare its halting ruggedness to
the fairy music of "The Day-Dream?"
Only the people who profess to like the
Venus of Milo better without her lost
arms than with them—the people to whom
deficiency and inadequacy are held dearer
than flawlessness and finish. A passion
for Mr. Browning's work has frequently
been one of the refuges of mediocrity.
You are thrown, as it were, with a mixed
but rather patrician society of, let us say
. . . invalids, in the same asylum. And it
is such a mild, elegant sort of lunacy!
Nobody is very much in earnest, after all.
They have learned, most of them, to look
as if they thought "A Pillar at Sebzevat"
luminiferous reading and "Jochanan Hak-
kadosh" a model of perspicuity. If you
say to them that Mr. Browning has never
produced a poem half so grand as the
"Ode on the Duke of Wellington," they
appear to feel so sorry for you that you
begin to feel sorry, yourself, for having
drawn thus largely, if unintentionally,
upon the funds of their compassion. And

yet bid them to show you where, throughout all Mr. Browning's dramatic idyls,
dramatic lyrics and dramatic everything
else, there are poems that so burn with
beauty as the monologues of " Œnone," of
" Tithonus," of " The Miller's Daughter,"
of " Maud," of " The Dream of Fair Women," of " The Palace of Art," of " St. Sim-
eon Stylites," of " The Gardener's Daughter," of " Sir Galahad," and they will be
apt to give you response as indefinite as if
it had been taken from some of their great
master's verse. For all these poems just
mentioned are monologues ; all, in varying
degrees, are essentially dramatic. Tennyson chose, until his later life, to ignore
the writing of drama ; but if he had attempted, in the full flush of his masterly
vigor, to produce a " Cup," a " Harold" or
a " Queen Mary," there cannot be much
real question as to whether he would or
would not have eclipsed "Colombe's Birthday " and " King Victor and King Charles."
I can ill imagine how any actual artist
would not instantly make up his mind to
retain "In Memoriam " and " The Princess " (those two inestimable marvels) even
if by doing so he were threatened with the
loss of everything that Mr. Browning has

ever done, from the murky glooms of
"Sordello" down to the recent most indo-
lently scribbled "Parleyings." And as for
those four incomparable "Idyls of the
King"—"Enid," "Elaine," Vivien" and
"Guinevere"—where amid the bristling
entanglements of such verse as that published by the author of "Prince Hohen-
stiel-Schwangau" shall we reach either
their peers or their semblances?

Scientific criticism, which is the only
kind meriting both credence and respect,
will one day, perhaps, demonstrate much
of what I have here only postulated, without aspiring logically to prove. And when
such an event occurs it should strike a telling blow at the languor which enervates a
large proportion of those readers who have
permitted their tastes to play very fantastic tricks with them. There is no objection to the hottest rebellion against purity
and sanity of method among iconoclasts
who would replace gentle order by dangerous misrule ; it is only when anarchy
gets into the high places of literature and
begins its assaults, mutilations and sub-
versions there that the intemperate are
led to exult and the judicious to deplore.
Still, progress, that arrives at so many of

her destinations by circuitous paths, may be trusted yet again to set the crooked straight. It deserves to be held as probable that she is at the present date mystically concerning herself with a future demolition of the " Browning Craze ; " and that her action may be speedy is a likelihood which all consistent optimists ought to place well up on the list of their rosiest hopes.

THE TRUTH ABOUT OUIDA.

READERS of current literature may have recently observed that two writers of reputation, Miss Harriet W. Preston and Mr. Julian Hawthorne, have been expressing rather pronounced opinions regarding the works of Ouida. Mr. Hawthorne's judgment was brief, and I need only add that it was extremely severe—far more severe, indeed, than any critical statement which I ever remember to have seen expressed by that writer. Miss Preston's decision took a much ampler form, and occupied nearly twelve pages of the *Atlantic Monthly*. Whatever may have been Miss Preston's intention, she certainly does not appeal to us as one whom the merits of Ouida have more than lukewarmly affected. And yet, at the beginning of her essay, she assumes the attitude of an appreciator rather than a detractor, taking pains to declare that her inquiry regarding the true causes of Ouida's immense popularity shall be " primarily

148

and chiefly a search for merits rather than
a citation of defects." With this excellent
resolution fully formed, she at once proceeds to draw comparisons between Ouida
and such great writers as Scott, George
Sand, and even Victor Hugo. This has an
encouraging sound enough ; we have the
sensation that a refreshingly new note is to
be struck in the general tone of fierce
vituperation by which Ouida has been so
persistently assailed for twenty years. The
truth about Ouida would be a pleasant
thing to hear; we have heard so much facile
falsehood. But Miss Preston proceeds to
invest her theme with a curiously languid
and tepid atmosphere. She finally aston-
ishes all the sincere admirers of Ouida—
and their number is to-day, among intelligent people, thousands and thousands—by
saying that her "imagination, vigorous
though it be and prolific, seldom rises to
really poetic heights." This is certainly
depressing for any one who has taken delight in such exceptional prose-poems as
"Ariadne" and "Signa." Still, a proper
avoidance of enthusiasm must always form
part of the modern critic's equipment ; the
fashion is to look at everything imperturb-
ably, from the Sphinx to the Brooklyn

Bridge ; we somehow only tolerate the ex-
orbitant and the florid when it takes the
shape of disgusted invective. For a long
period Ouida has endured the latter (not
always quite patiently, if some of her retali-
atory newspaper letters are recalled), and I
confess that we owe Miss Preston a debt of
gratitude for breaking the ice at last. None
the less, however, do we own to a feeling
that the ice might have been assailed by a
little heavier and more efficient cleaver.
The *Atlantic* reviewer appears, indeed, to
be a trifle afraid, not to say ashamed, of
her own pioneership. Tradition would
seem to be furtively reminding her that she
is heading a revolt against it. And there
certainly might well seem a kind of literary
defiance in any defence of Ouida. She has
stood so long as a pariah that to give her
boldly a few credentials of respectabilty, as
it were, might in a temperament by no
means timid still require some courage. I
would not even appear to suggest that Miss
Preston has doubted her own assertions
concerning this great romancist, whenever
they have been of a favorable turn. But it
has struck me that she has almost doubted
the advisability of her own position as so
distinct a non-conformist. One smiles to

remember the ridiculous abuse poured upon
Ouida in England ever since somewhere
about the year 1863. She has probably
afforded more opportunity for the callow
undergraduate satirist than any author of
the present century. I do not maintain that
she was at first the recipient of an unde-
served ridicule. But afterward this ridicule, because of the radical change in her
work, became pitiably tell-tale ; it revealed
that aggravating conservatism in those who
arraigned her which had its root in either
a very unjust, hasty and perfunctory skim-
ming of her later books, or an entire ignorance of their contents. She undoubtedly
began all wrong. There are some liberal
and high-minded people with whom the
follies and faults of such stories as " Granville de Vigne" and "Idalia" have wrought
so disastrously that all their future impressions have been colored by these uncon-
querable associations. It seems to me that
Mr. Hawthorne is one of these, and I am
certain that the late Bayard Taylor was
one. When "Ariadne" appeared, only a
year or two before Taylor's lamentably ill-
timed death, he wrote concerning that en-
chanting tale in the New York *Tribune* with
a sternness of condemnation most regret-

table, as I thought, in so alert and vigorous
an intellect. When I expressed to Taylor
my surprise that he should have seen nothing beautiful or poetic in "Ariadne," he
frankly declared to me that he saw nothing
commendable in any line that Ouida had
written. But many of her lovely sketches
had already appeared, and that exquisite
idyl, " Bébée, or The Two Little Wooden
Shoes," with its tearful tenderness and its
fiery, gloomy, piercing *finale* of passion, had
given proof of its author's wakening force
and discipline.

Miss Preston's chief error, I should affirm,
has been her somewhat careless huddling
together of all Ouida's works and passing
criticism upon them *en bloc*, without more
than vague indication of the different peri-
ods in which they were produced, or the
various stages of development which they
exhibit. This talented lady, however she
is to be praised for taking Ouida seriously
(and that is a fine thing to have done at all,
when it meant the flinging down of a
gauntlet before disparagement no less in-
sensate than cruel), has still failed in taking
Ouida half seriously enough. I read with
astonishment in the *Atlantic* review, for example, an extended notice of "Idalia,"

while such vastly better work as " Folle-
Farine" or " In Maremma" was quietly ig-
nored. Candidly, I hold that Miss Preston's
entire consideration of Ouida has been as
limited, unsatisfactory and insufficient as,
when all circumstantial points are duly
recognized, it has been kindly, generous,
and honorable.

I have already expressed it as my conviction that Ouida began very badly. She
indeed began‾ as badly as any genius did
whose early and subsequent accomplish-
ments in English letters are now known to
us and may be read side by side with hers.
Byron certainly showed far less power at
the commencement of his career than she
did at the commencement of hers ; and
those who possess my own deep veneration
for the grandeur of Tennyson's poetry at
its highest heights may have read some of
the deplorable stanzas, modelled on a sort
of hideous German-English plan, which
have thus far, I believe, escaped the savage
exposures of even his most merciless American publishers. I find myself involuntarily
tracing a parallel between the young Ouida
and the young poets who preceded her by
a few decades more or less. But this tendency easily explains itself, since she is pre-

eminently a poet, notwithstanding her great
gifts for romantic narration. The rhythmic
faculty has been denied her, and for this
reason she probably has written so much
of that " poetical prose" which the average
Englishman has been taught to hold in
such phlegmatic contempt. If " Granville
de Vigne", had appeared in rhymes as clever
and as prolix as Owen Meredith's " Lucile,"
it would doubtless have won a place far
above that bright, hybrid, pseudo-poetic
popular favorite. But " Granville de Vigne"
has won no place, nor has "Strathmore,"
nor has " Idalia," nor has " Puck," nor even
" Chandos," pronounced as was the dawn-
ing change it exhibited. These works all
mean a palæozoic age for Ouida : her extraordinary powers were yet struggling for
worthier expression. They are valuable
alike in their absurdities and their better
revelations, though the latter shone fitful,
indeterminate, and often distressingly transient. The superabundance of " color," the
weight of adjective piled on adjective, the
lavish display of an erudition as voluminous as it was sometimes erratic, the meretricious defects of style, the *collet monté*
superfluity of rhetoric, the impossible and
ludicrous descriptions of luxury—all this

has become with many of us in a manner
comically classic. Ouida's early heroes,
with their fleet Arabian steeds, their lordly
lineage, their fabulous wealth or sentiment-
ally picturesque poverty, their fatal fascina-
tions for women and their deadly muscular
developments for men — Ouida's early
heroes, I say, have grown as representative
of the overwrought in fiction as those of
Byron have grown representative of like in-
discretion in poetry. Nor are these faults
of her youth entirely outlived by Ouida.
" Fine writing" is still occasionally her
bane, though it becomes less and less so
with each new book she now produces. Her
vocabulary has always been as copious as
the sunlight itself, and her style is at present a direct, flexible and notably elegant
one. She has been accused of "cramming,"
and of making a little knowledge do service for much. But only very illiterate
people could believe such a masquerade
possible with her. She is indisputably a
woman of spacious and most diversified
learning, though she has not always known
either the art of modestly concealing this
fact, or that of letting it speak spontane-
ously and judiciously for itself. Still,
pedantry is not seldom the attribute of a

greatly cultivated mind. We have seen this in the case of George Eliot, whose admirers will perhaps feel like mobbing me when they read that I think her genius in many ways inferior to that of Ouida. And yet I grant that to a very large extent she possesses what Ouida was for a long time almost totally without—taste, artistic patience, and that surest of preservatives, a firm and chiselled style.

"Under Two Flags" may be said to have recorded a turning-point in this unique writer's career. It was full of the same tinselled and lurid hyperboles which had made so many readers of the extraordinary series hold up horrified hands in the past. But its gaudiness and opulence of language were suited to its Algerian *locale*, and the drowsy palms and deep-blue African skies of which it spoke to us accorded with the tropic tendencies of its phrases. It displayed a wondrous acquaintance, also, with military life in Algeria, and for this reason amazed certain observers of an altered *mise en scène* in a novelist whom they had believed only able to misrepresent the patrician circles of England. But "Under Two Flags" amazed by its perusal from still another cause. It contained one of

the most thrillingly dramatic episodes ever
introduced into any novel of the school to
which such episodes belong, namely, the
wild desert journey of Cigarette, the *vivan-
dière*, bearing a pardon for the condemned
soldier whom she loves. Cigarette reaches
the place of execution just in time to fling
herself upon her lover's breast and save
him from the bullets of his foes by dying
under them. We are apt nowadays to look
askance at such heroic incidents, and the
word "unnatural" easily rises to our lips
as we do so. Perhaps it rises there too
easily. Self-sacrifice of the supreme kind
has gone out of fashion in modern story-
telling, and by a tacit surrender we have
given scenes like this, with all their warm-
blooded kinships, to the domain of the
theatre. That fiction will ever care to re-
sume her slighted prerogative, the thriving
influence of Zola and his more moderate
American imitators would lead us to believe
improbable. Still, the caprices of popular
demand lend themselves unwillingly to
prophecy. One fact, however, cannot plaus-
ibly be contradicted: the theatre has not
invested her gift at any very profitable rate
of interest, nor justified her present mono-
poly of all that is stirring in romanticism.

"Tricotrin," if I mistake not, was the first important successor of "Under Two Flags," and here Ouida gave us the noteworthy proof that she had turned her attention toward ideal and poetic models. I fear it must be chronicled that the chaff in "Tricotrin" predominates over the wheat. The whole story is not seldom on stilts, and we often lose patience with the hero as more of a *poseur* than of the demigod he is described. The entire *donnée* is too high-strung for its nineteenth-century concomitance. We feel as if everybody should wear what the managers of theatres would call "shape dresses." Ouida still tempts the parodist ; the machinery of her plot, so to speak, almost creaks with age, now and then ; her personages attitudinize and are often tiresomely verbose. Tricotrin does so much with the aid of red fire and a calcium that his glaringly melodramatic death becomes almost a relief in the end. And yet the book scintillates with brilliant things, and if it had been written with an equal power in French instead of English, might have passed for the work of Victor Hugo. There is a great deal about it that the passionate and democratic soul of the French poet would have cordially delighted

in. It belongs to the same quaiity of inspiration that produced "Notre Dame de
Paris," "L'Homme Qui Rit," and "Fan-
tine." But there have always been English
people who have laughed at Hugo's tales,
and in much the same spirit Ouida's coun-
trymen laughed at the itinerant, commu-
nistic Tricotrin, with his superb beauty, his
pastoral abstemiousness and purity, his altruistic philanthropy, his forsworn birth-
right of an English earl, his wide *clientèle* of
grimy and outcast worshippers, and his as-
tounding range of opportunity to appear
just in the nick of time and succor the op-
pressed. Far more daring license with the
manipulation of fact, however, has been
taken by the elder Dumas and others.
Ouida's book came about thirty or forty
years too late for sober critical acceptance
in her own country, and it was of a kind
that her own country has never perma-
nently accepted. Still, it revealed her perhaps for the first time as an original power
in letters. She had struck in it the one
note which has always been most positively
her own ; she had told the world that she
was a prose-poet of dauntless imagination
and solitary excellence. As an idealist in
prose fiction no English writer has thus far

approached her. "Tricotrin" would not
alone have made her what she is. It remained for her to improve upon this remarkable effort, and to fling up, like some
tract of land under convulsive disturbance,
peaks that for height and splendor far out-
rivalled it. The valleys in her literary
landscape are sometimes low indeed ; a few
even have noxious growths in them, and
are haunted by foolish wills-o'-the-wisp.
Such, I should say, are her first few sus-
tained works, like "Granville de Vigne"
and "Strathmore." Nor has she always
clung to the talisman by which she afterward learned to invoke her best creations.
At times she has seemed to cast this temporarily away, as in "Friendship" and
"A Winter City." I have now reached, as
it were, my one sole conclusion regarding
her abilities at their finest and securest
outlook. She is an idealist, and that she
should have determinedly remained. The
foibles of modern society are no subjects
for either her dissection or her satire. She
has never been any more able to become a
Thackeray or a Dickens than they, under
any conceivable circumstances, could have
become Ouidas. It is an immense thing
for a writer to recognize just what he is

capable of doing best, and to leave all the
rest alone. But Ouida, with a burning un-
easiness, has continually misunderstood her
own noble gifts. With an eye that could
look undimmed at the sun, she has too
often grown weary of his beams. Once
sure of her wings, white and strong as they
proved, she had nothing to seek except the
soft welcome of the air for which they
were so buoyantly fitted. But no : she has
repeatedly folded them and walked instead
of flying. Birds that fly with grace do not
often walk so. She is a poet, and she has
forgotten this truth with a pertinacity
which has been a deprivation to the literature of her time. And yet for several years
after the publication of "Tricotrin" the
idealist was most hopefully paramount in
all that she did. If "Folle-Farine" had
been her first book instead of her sixth or
seventh, it would have made even the English blood that she has more than once declared so sluggish, tingle with glad appreciation of its loveliness. The change in her
was for a time absolute and thorough.
"Folle-Farine" was the story of a despised
outcast girl, ignorant and unlettered, yet
with a soul quick to estimate and treasure
the worth and meaning of beauty wherever

found.   It is all something which the realists would pull long faces or giggle at as
hopelessly "highfalutin."   But then the
realists, when they ride their hobby with a
particularly martial air, are inclined quite
to trample all poetry below its hoofs.   I
don't know how well the story of "Folle-
Farine" would please some of Balzac's successors, but I am sure that he himself would
have delighted in it.   The girl's infancy
among the gypsies and subsequent fierce
persecution at the hands of her grandfather,
Claudis Flamma, as one devil-begotten and
loathsome, are treated with an intensity
bordering on the painful.   But through all
the youthful anguish and martyrdom of
"Folle-Farine" there flows a charming
current of idyllic feeling.   Such passages
as these, stamped with the individuality
of Ouida, meet us on every page : "In
one of the most fertile and fair districts of
Northern France there was a little Norman
town, very, very old, and beautiful exceedingly by reason of its ancient streets, its
high peaked roofs, its marvellous galle-
ries and carvings, its exquisite grays and
browns, its silence and its color, and its
rich still life.   Its centre was a great cathedral, noble as York or Chartres ; a cathedral

whose spire shot to the clouds, and whose
innumerable towers and pinnacles were all
pierced to the day, so that the blue sky shone
and the birds of the air flew all through
them. A slow brown river, broad enough
for market-boats and for corn-barges, stole
through the place to the sea, lapping as it
went the wooden piles of the houses, and
reflecting the quaint shapes of the carvings,
the hues of the signs and the draperies, the
dark spaces-of the dormer windows, the
bright heads of some casement-cluster of
carnations, the laughing face of a girl lean-
ing out to smile on her lover."

This certainly is not what we call com-
pact writing; there is none of that neat-
ness and trimness about it which bespeak
the deliberative pen or the compunctious
eraser. But what a sensuous and winsome
poetic effect does it produce ! Few writers
can afford the loose clauses, the random
laissez-aller, of Ouida. She sometimes
abuses her assumed privilege, even in her
most authentic moments—those, I mean,
of pure imagination. But it is then that
the superabundance of her diction and its
careless yet shining fluency hardly ever lose
their attractiveness. It is then that the
prolixity to which I have before referred is

an attribute we are glad to pardon, and
love while we are doing so.   The argument
of " Folle-Farine" soon ceases to deal with
the sufferings of a child.   The poor creature's hopeless love for the cold and unconsciously heedless Arslàn, bitter at the
world's indifference to those magnificent
gods and goddesses that he still goes on
painting in his old granary among water-
docks and rushes there by the river-side,
is portrayed with unnumbered masterly
strokes.   And afterward, when Folle-Farine
tends him as he lies stricken with fever in
a Parisian attic, the evil temptings of the
unprincipled Sartorian, as they offer life
and fame to Arslàn at a price whose infamy
cannot be questioned by her who hears
them, cloud this whole narrative with a
truly terrible gloom.   Folle-Farine's immo-
lation of self to save him whom she worships, and her final self-inflicted death amid
the peace of the river-reeds, far away from
the loud and gilded Paris that she detests,
are the very darkest essence of the most
absorbing and desolating tragedy.   But
the poetry of this whole fervid conception
is never once lost sight of.   We close the
book with a shudder, as if we had been
passing through the twilight of some magic

forest where the dews are death. But we realize how matchless is the sorcery that can so sombrely enchain us, and long after its woful spell has vanished memory vibrates with the pity and sorrow it roused.

"Ariadne" is another masterpieee, and not unlike the foregoing in the main sources of its excessive melancholy. It is the story of a feminine spirit swayed by an unreciprocated love, as waywardly given as lightly undervalued. The characters are without subtlety, as in all Ouida's prose-poems. They are fascinating or repelling shadows, whom we can name adoration, egotism, fidelity, as we please, but whose eerie juxtapositions, whose pictorial and half-illusory surroundings, may summon sensations not unlike those caused in us by some admirable yet faded fresco. Never was Rome, in all her grandeur and desuetude, made the more majestic background of a heart's forlorn history. We read of "the silver lines of the snow new-fallen on the mountains against the deep rose of dawn;" of how "shadows of the night steal softly from off the city, releasing, one by one, dome and spire and cupola and roof, till all the wide white wonder of the place ennobles itself under the broad brightness of full day ;" of how one can "go down into the dark cool streets, with the pigeons flutter- ing in the fountains, and the sounds of the morning chants coming from many a church door and convent window, and little schol- ars and singing-children going by with white clothes on, or scarlet robes, as though walking forth from the canvas of Botticelli or Garofalo." Sculpture forms what one might call the pervading stimulus of this most impassioned story, its young heroine being a sculptor of inspired powers. In the same way music supplies an incessant ac- companiment for the glowing words of "Signa." The youth who gives his name to the book is a musician who possesses something more glorious than mere apti- tude. Psychologically it is the reverse of "Ariadne," delineating the torment of a man who puts faith in the most shallow and vacant female nature. It is just as plaintive, just as haunting, as its prede- cessor, but it is simpler, less penetrative and less wide-circling, less Dantesque in its mournful dignity and less astonishing through its scholarship. These three prose- poems, " Folle-Farine," " Ariadne " and " Signa," are the three high alps of Ouida's accomplishment thus far. It is not easy

to praise them with full justice, because
unrestrained panegyric is never that, and
yet the lyrical spontaneity of the works
themselves—their evidence of having won
their splendid vitality by having been
poured from the writer's inmost heart, as
warm as that heart's blood—would tempt
one who had fully felt their strength, orig-
inality and greatness, to dip his pen in exceedingly rosy ink and then shape with it
very ardent encomiums. I am far from calling these memorable undertakings "idyls,"
as Miss Preston terms them, or in any manner agreeing that " Friendship " "marks a
distinct intellectual advance."

Here was a woman who had shown us as
no one else, living or dead, ever had shown
in precisely the same way, that she could
make the sweetest and most impressive
poetry do service as the medium for telling
the sweetest and most impressive of tales.
Mixed with their Gothic fantasy there was
something Homeric in these three volumes
which I have before named. There were
no touches that reminded us at all of the
modern novel. Each had its separate
æsthetic haze clinging about it, and a golden
haze this was, in every case. With only a
few changes here and there, the atmosphere

of each story might have been made Greek,
or even Egyptian. The delights or horrors
of life were put most strikingly under our
vision; but the details of life, the routine
of things *au jour le jour*, the trifling modes
and customs of mortality, as it pursues its
whims, its vices, its flirtations, its amours,
its divorce-suits, all remained remote and
unconsidered. The glamour of dream clung
to every character and event. The joys and
miseries outrolled before us were as abstract
and aloof, when viewed with relation to our
morning mail or our menaced butcher's-
bill, as the loves of Paris and Helen in the
Iliad, or of Ulysses and Calypso in the
Odyssey. These three enticing stories no
more concerned our bread-and-butter-get-
ting existences of prosaic actuality than
they concerned the wash of tides at either
pole. We turned their glowing leaves to
escape from our own silent quarrel with
realities rather than to meet the monoto-
nous recurrence of them either photographed
painstakingly or sketched felicitously. In
other words, we gave ourselves up to the
alternately gentle or stormy wizardries of
a poet, contented in the oblivion thus begotten for decorated statistics of the annal-
ist or placid vivisections of the surgeon.

I am aware that all such departure from
his cherished modern standards must at
once be tyrannously cried down as a bore
by that self-satisfied arbiter, the average
reader of to-day. Perhaps Ouida felt some
necessity of propitiating this multiform
custodian of profit and loss. It may have
been that her publishers told her, with that
sincere sadness born of financial depression,
how much handsomer had been the " re-
turns" from " Strathmore" and "Chandos"
than from "Ariadne" or "Signa." Be this
as it may, Ouida forsook her new gods, and,
except in the composition of some exquisite
short pieces which recalled the purity, the
human breadth and the past star-like ra-
diance of "A Provence Rose," "A Dog of
Flanders" and " The Nürnberg Stove," I
do not know of her having ever again hewn
her statues from the same flawless Pentelic
marble.

But the resumption of her old more materialistic task—that of writing novels
which should reflect the doings and misdo-
ings of her own century—she was now prepared to undertake with a much firmer
hand and with an unquestionably chastened
sense of old delinquencies. The tale
" Friendship" may be said to commemorate

this unfortunate transition. It marks the third distinct change in Ouida's mental posture toward her public. It is to me a descent and not an elevation, and yet I freely concede that the novelist *rediviva* was in every way superior to the novelist who lived and rhapsodized before. In " Friend-ship" we see much of the flare and glare once thrown upon every-day occurrences tempered to a far more tolerable light. Deformity often takes the lines of just pro-portion, and not seldom of amiable sym-metry as well. Miss Preston praises " Friendship" as pre-eminently readable in every part, and here I should again differ from her, since in my judgment the book contains a great deal of insufferable tedium. Ouida's worst fault as a stylist is here laid tormentingly bare. She harps with such stress of repetition upon the guilty bondage of Prince Ioris to Lady Joan Challoner that the perpetual circumlocution makes a kind of maëlstrom in which interest becomes at last remorselessly swallowed. It has been stated that incidents and characters in " Friendship" were taken from Ouida's own life, and that Lady Joan Challoner's name conceals one belonging to a foe of the au-thor. Whether this report be true or false,

we resent the almost maliciously periphras-
tic style in which we are told again and
again that Lady Joan was the jailer of Ioris
and watched him struggle in vain with the
gyves of his own sin. To have a nature of
the most detestable selfishness described
over and over till we are familiar with its
meanest impulse, its narrowest spite, resembles being seated by a person of repulsive physiognomy in a chamber lined with
mirrors. The reduplications become un-
bearable to us; till we take the only feasible
course for avoiding them: we go into another apartment. Still, in the present case,
I did not go into another apartment; I fin-
ished "Friendship," and received from it an
impression as vivid as disagreeable. *C'est
le ton qui fait la musique,* and this story, notwithstanding its eternity of repetitions,
appeared to me told in a querulous, railing
voice which robbed it of charm. But it
evinces a most undeniable improvement in
method. The sentences are terser and
crisper than in those other adolescent novels, and the syntax is no longer straggling
and hazardous. Of a certain redundancy
Ouida has never wholly rid herself. The
effort to do so is manifest in her later books,
but it still remains a weakness with her to

tell us the same thing a number of times,
and with only a comparative alteration of
phraseology. Still, no one—not even Balzac himself—has a more succinct, dry,
poignant way of putting epigram. It seems
to me that she is without humor ; her fun
inevitably stings as wit alone can do ; that
soft phosphorescent play of geniality which
would try to set its reflex gleam in the
stony gaze of a gorgon, appears quite unknown to her. She has been wise, too, in
not cultivating humor, for it is something
which must fall upon a writer from heaven :
he might as well try and train himself into
having blue eyes instead of black. But
Ouida has trained many of her qualities, and
the self-search with which she has done so
has betokened the most scourge-like rigors.
The novelist in her is to me all a matter of
talent vigilantly guarded and nurtured ;
the poetic part of her—the part to which
we are indebted for three supreme achievements—could not have helped delivering
its beautiful message. Afterward Ouida
remembered that she was somebody quite
outside of what one would call a genius —
that she was a woman of enormously ver-
satile information, and that the possibility
of her writing novels which would excite a

great deal of public attention could scarcely
be overestimated. Beyond doubt she had
now reached a state of dexterity as regarded
mere craftsmanship which thoroughly
eclipsed the crudity of former times. But
just as she had been raw and experimental
in a way quite her own, so was she now
adroit, self-restrained and professional with
a similar freshness.

"Moths" came next, and was a book
sought and commented upon, admired and
execrated, from St. Petersburg to San Francisco. Of all her novels, this is perhaps
the one which has brought her the greatest
number of readers in what may be set down
as the third period of her singular celebrity.
It is filled with the most drastic interest
for even the most jaded and *ennuyé* exam-
iner. The story is the perfection of enter-
tainment, of diversion. Its sarcastic scorn
of fashionable frailties and flippancies even
surpasses that which made "Friendship"
notorious. Social life among the most
aristocratic people of Europe is drawn so
sumptuously and prismatically that without ever having enjoyed the honor of din-
ing or supping with princes and duchesses,
we still own to a secret revolt against the
verisimilitude of their recorded pastimes

and dissipations. In "Moths," as in all her purely fictional and unpoetic work, Ouida gives us the belief that she is flying her kite entirely too high, that she is too greatly enamoured of the rank and titles of her dukes and earls, that the European *beau monde*, as an idea, has too bewilderingly intoxicated her fancy. As Balzac delighted in letting us know the exact number of francs per annum possessed by almost every member of his *Comédie Humaine*, so Ouida loves to tell us of her grandees' castles and palaces, of their *fêtes* and *musicales*, of their steam-yachts and their four-in-hands, of their "private physicians" (it is rarely one simple physician with her), of their multitudinous retainers and servants. Her heroines go to their apartments to dress, and in so doing give themselves up to their "women:" it is seldom that any one of them is humbly enough placed to have merely a single *femme de chambre*. All the horses are blooded animals, all the jewels priceless, all the repasts miracles of gastronomy, all the ladies' toilets royally costly. Saloons and boudoirs and bedchambers are adorned with wonders of modern art, on canvas or in marble, in tapestry or bric-à-brac, in panellings or frescos. Nearly every new book that she writes is a sort of *édition de luxe* of itself. I am by no means sure that she does not smile at the dazzling glories which she evokes, while continuing to spread them before us with a secret conviction that they will allure hundreds and even thousands, though they repel tens and twenties, of those whom they confront. What to many refined observers may have seemed a streak of trivial childishness in her may be, after all, a shrewder cleverness than these accredit her with. For Ouida is superlatively clever ; indeed, it may be added by those whom none of her sham glitterings have blinded to the genuineness of her actual gold, that she is lamentably clever. Had she thought less of a certain transient applause which writers incomparably beneath her may win, she might much sooner have attained that firm fame during her lifetime which her death alone will now create. In " Moths" the cleverness to which I have alluded is everywhere apparent. She has made it a story that the shop-girl or the dry-goods clerk may read with thrills and tears. Vera's horrible misfortune in having been sold by her mother to the brutish Russian prince admits of no misinterpreta-

tion. The vast command of wealth and
the lofty station which now follow for
the dreamy and statuesque heroine are skil-
fully blended with her love for the brilliant
marquis-tenor Corrèze and the distressing
captivity of her jewelled chains. There is
a strong suggestion of the "penny dread-
fuls" in the whole *entourage* of the tale,
with Vera's anguished heart beating under
robes of velvet and her tortured brain
throbbing under coronets of gems. But it
is immeasurably above the vulgarity of
those gaudy and often mawkish serials.
Its pathos is intense, and its continuous
intervals of pure poetry are undeniable. It
is dramatic, too, in the very strictest sense,
and its adaptation for the English stage
was naturally to be expected. As for what
the moralists would call its "lesson," I
should affirm that to be exempt from the
least chance of misconstruction. Like all
these later stories of Ouida's, "Moths" has
been denounced as grossly unwholesome
for young minds. I do not know about
young minds gaining benefit from its perusal; I should imagine that, like many
things which minors do not understand, its
effect upon them might be harmful, and
even noxious. So is the effect of rich

dishes and indigestible fruit upon young
stomachs, while stronger gastric juices
sustain no hurt from their consumption.
It is time that this outcry against what is
evil in literature for young minds should
be silenced by a sensible consideration of
how potent or impotent are the defences
reared by educators and guardians. It
would surely be unwise to cut down all the
apple-orchards because in those days which
precede autumn's due ripeness multitudes
of foraging children have brought on themselves avoidable colics. If the colics sleep
in the undeveloped apples, and mischievous little Adams and Eves *will* taste thereof,
a stout wall and an ill-tempered dog behind
it are the only trustworthy preventives
against their temerity. To claim that
Ouida's works are not healthful reading
for those whose youth makes the mere
mention of evil and vice deleterious because in all their bad meanings unexplain-
able, is to claim, I think, that any author
may be misunderstood provided the mentality of his public is sufficiently meagre
for his miscomprehension. The decried
"immorality" of Ouida I have never at all
been able to perceive. I ignore the question of her immoral purport in the prose-

poems heretofore treated. There such a
discussion wears colors of absurdity; it is
almost as if some one should assure me
Milton's Satan was a matter of shame to
his portrayer. But with regard to all
Ouida's novels of what I have called her
third period, the accusation (and it is a
very wide accusation) becomes at least
worthy of attention. Ouida has no hesitation in referring to relations between the
sexes which common conventionality has
reprobated and condemned. A great deal
of her more modern work deals frankly with
this theme. Sometimes it is dealt with in
tones and terms of a most scathing irony;
again it is handled with mixed disdain and
ridicule; and still again it is openly grieved
over and deplored. But I fail to find a
single instance of the vileness of adultery
being either condoned or alleviated. To
choose an uncanny subject is very different
from handling the subject with the grosser
motive of extenuating what is base in it.
I should assert that Ouida never—absolutely never—does the latter. There are
one or two scenes in " Moths " which have
a shocking nudity of candor. But they
are never dwelt upon for the purpose of
pandering to any despicable taste in the

reader. They form a link in the dolorous chain-work of the heroine's ills, and they are introduced for the purpose of render-ing her final step of rebellion against the world's legally imposed pressure more pardonably consistent with the whole scheme of her unsolicited mishaps. While revealing what she believes to be low and contemptible in society of to-day, Ouida employs merely the weapons which Juvenal himself made use of. She is never sympa-thetic with wrong-doing, any more than the Latin poet was in fulminating against Roman decadence. Witness, as an exam-ple of this impersonal sincerity, her un-sparing denunciations hurled at such char-acters as Lady Joan in "Friendship" and Lady Dolly in "Moths." How cordially she seems to detest the artificiality of ev-ery *mauvais sujet* she describes ! She lays bare alike the sordid and the sensual aim; she pierces with her shafts of wit and hate the adventurer, the hypocrite, the scandal-monger, the titled voluptuary, the menda-cious and guileful male flirt, the modest-visaged and still more deceptive *intrigante.* But through all her *danse macabre* of ill-behaved people there is no revelation which may even faintly indicate that she is in any

way sympathetic with their indiscreet or
reckless caperings. For those who shout
Ouida down as abominable because she
chooses to touch the abominable, I have
no answer. All that point of view merely
involves the question of whether the abominable can be touched or not in literature,
provided it is so approached and so grasped
that the author makes its mirk and stain
seem nothing but the soilure and grossness
which they really are. I am acquainted
with several American men of letters who
have told me that they deeply regret the
broad public distaste for so-called "in-
decency" in novel-writing. These men
have already written novels of merit and
force, but they greatly desire to write novels which may express the full scope and
depth of life as they see and feel it. They
declare themselves, however, debarred from
such performance by the stringent edicts
of their publishers and editors. It seems
to me that Ouida has quietly contemned
the inclinations of her publishers and editors. She has chosen to tell the whole
truth—not as Zola tells it, but as George
Sand (whom she resembles in one way as
much as she resembles Victor Hugo in
another) always chose uncompromisingly

to tell it. Her gorgeousness of surrounding has made her perfectly pure and reformatory motive dim to those who cannot eliminate from the scum and reek of a stagnant pool the iridescence filmed there. Ouida has seen the rainbow colors close-clinging to such malodorous torpor in human society, and she has striven to report of them as faithfully as of the brackish waters below. But she has intensified their baleful tints. She has made the ermine that wraps her sinful potentates too white and the black spots which indent this ermine too inky. She is and has always been incapable of saying to her muse what Mr. Lowell says in his profound though pietistic poem, " The Cathedral:"

> " Oh, more than half-way turn that Grecian front
> Upon me, while with half-rebuke I spell,
> On the plain fillet that confines thy hair
> In conscious bounds of seeming unconstraint,
> The *Naught in overplus*, thy race's badge !"

No; Ouida determinedly delights in overplus, and when one thinks of her muse at all it is of a harried and overtaxed muse, with feverish imprecations against the wear and tear to which divinity has been heartlessly subjected. When I turn toward the

novels which have succeeded "Moths," I
am constrained to declare Ouida a writer
more fertile in expedients for disillusioning
her most loyal adherents than any other
known through the past centuries as one
deserving the name of a genius. (She is so
incontestably a genius, however, that she
can go on committing her excesses without
alienating her leal devotees.) She is like
some monarch confident of his subjects'
worship while he crowns himself with roses
and quaffs wine from gold beakers to the
detriment and discontent of throngs waiting at his gates.   There are no throngs
waiting at Ouida's gates, however ; or
rather the throngs are her entranced readers, and not by any means those fastidious
about the requirements of true royalty.
But a few, knowing her grand mind, regret the self-forgetfulness to which it has
stooped.

"In Maremma" startled these few, as
if it were a pledge of permanent return
among the classic idealisms which have
made this author's best right to assert herself one of the greatest figures in contem-
porary literature.   And "In Maremma" is
a tale of matchless grace and sweetness.
We marvel as we read of the Italian girl

who went and dwelt in the Etruscan tomb,
loving the dead whom she found buried
there, and finally meeting in it, by a most
terrible satire of circumstances, him who
dealt her a death-wound of passion—we
marvel, I say, as we read of this delicious,
free-souled, innocent kinswoman to Folle-
Farine and Ariadne, how any human brain
could be so multiplex and many-shaded as
that of Ouida. What gulfs of difference
separate this new heroine of hers from
the world-encompassed and society-beset
beings whom she has so recently pictured !
And yet for a time the novelist has dropped
her microscope (often so foolishly misem-
ployed) and the poet has resumed her
neglected lyre. Their old notes are still
struck with dulcet harmony. "In Maremma" is Ouida again at her loftiest and
most authentic. (She shows in it her old
impetuous desire to feel with and for the
persecuted and maltreated of the earth) I
cannot explain why it should not be ranked
with the three great masterpieces to which
I have already made such enthusiastic
reference. Pehaps it should be so ranked.
If there is any excuse for depriving it of a
place on this exquisite list, that excuse
must be found in its more earthly *raison*

d'être when compared with the almost ethe-
real spirituality of the other books.

"Wanda," "Princess Napraxine," and
"Othmar," coming afterward with a speed
of succession that showed the most earnest
industry, have given proof of their author's
second return to at least relative realism.
But "Wanda" is a romance of inexpressi-
ble grace and force. It is the purest romance: to speak of it as highly colored
is like calling a particularly rich sunset
overfraught with glows and tints. Judging
it by the modern methods of the "natural-
istic" school is to pronounce it a monstrosity
of art. But a great many of the elder Dumas's works would suffer in a like way if so
considered, and nearly every prose line of
Hugo's would fall under the same ban of dis-
favor. "Wanda" is a great romantic story.
Its mode of telling is one protracted intensity. Its fires burn with a raging and heavy-
odored flame. But they spring forth, for all
that, with no ungoverned madness. They
are kindled by a hand desirous of their
heat and curl but avoidant of their reckless outflow. It is very easy to denounce
such a tale as vulgar. In these final years
of our dying century all literary fierce-
ness and eagerness of this kind are so de-

nounced. If romanticism is to fade away forever, this volcanic bit of sensationalism is undoubtedly doomed. But its sensation-alism is of the sort we think of when we remind ourselves of "Monte Christo" and " Le Juif Errant." The haughty Austrian countess, with her prestige of stainless pedigree and her imperial self-esteem,— the Russian serf who has concealed his disgraceful birth under a stolen title,— the Hungarian nobleman of almost kingly rank and unblemished honor, who con-temptuously lays bare the shameful brand of imposture in his, rival,—the ancestral castle in the Tyrol, with obeisant swarms of vassals and its regal household admin-istration,—all these are the old materials and manœuvres of "Strathmore" and " Idalia," but presented with tenfold more adroitness and *savoir faire.* The secret of reading " Wanda" with the keenest relish for its exuberant ardors must lie in com-plete forgetfulness of life as it is and pious acceptance of life as it might be. But this is the test by which nearly all romance is tried. I have no space to treat at length of " Princess Napraxine " and its sequel, " Othmar ;" but if space were broadly al-lowed me I could state of them no more

and no less than I have already stated of
"Wanda." Princess Napraxine herself is
a silly and patience-taxing person. Ouida's
enemies must have exulted in her as "immoral," which she indeed truly would be
were she not so transparently *légère*. The
chief pity is that so fine a fellow as Othmar
should have done anything except disdain
her. But both these two last novels teem
with pages of description, reflection, tenderness, sweetness and pathos which make
the fact doubly sad that Princess Napraxine (a pedant, a prig and a strutting com-
bination of silliness and bad manners)
should ever have been summoned to blot
and mar them by her paltry charlatanisms.

The isolated position held by Ouida in an
age when principles and theories essentially
opposite to her own have seemingly cap-
tured the world of letters, would of itself
point to endowments both rare and sturdy.
That she has pushed her way into renown
against obstacles which were often all the
more stubborn because they were of her
own rearing, is a matter for serious inquiry
and reflection ; but that she should have
forced from certain able contemporaries
who originally satirized and flouted her,
the respect and homage which we pay to

transcendent competency, is a still more significant truth. It means that Ouida must mount to her place of deserved state in spite of faults which would shape for many another writer stairways with a wholly different direction. But there has seldom been a writer whose virtues and vices were so inextricably blended. For example, the very people, in her stories of fashionable society, who conduct themselves with the least lucid common-sense perpetually spice their repartees and railleries with a most engaging wit. We may not sympathize with what they say, but we are keenly amused by their modes of saying it. Disraeli, whom I believe Ouida sincerely admires as a novelist, possesses all her love for palatial filigree and porphyry ; yet he has nothing of her sprightliness, crispness and *verve* when telling us of the bores, the simpletons and the few passably bright people who make up "society."

In more than a single way Ouida is behind her time,—a time over whose rather barren-looking levels of analysis and formulation she flings the one large light of romance now visible. In this latter respect she is, indeed, a kind of glorious anachronism, but from another stand-point her

grooves of thought appear painfully narrow.   Occasionally she airs a contempt for
her own sex which makes us wish that with
all her learning she knew a little more of
the dispassionate repose taught by science,
and of its hardy feuds against reckless assumptions.   Ouida has made declarations
about womankind which cause us to wonder how she can possibly have been so unfortunate in her feminine friends, with the
thousands of chaste and lovable women
now to be met inside the limits of civilization.   The *mauvaise langue*, when turned
against womanhood, is nowadays classed
among effete frivolities.   What we forgave
at the beginning of the century, on this
head, we now simply dismiss as beneath
anything like grave heed.   The day has
passed when such Byronics of misogyny,
however gilt with flashing sarcasms, will
either delude or solace.   We leave "sneers
at the sex" to the idleness of otherwise
unemployed club-loungers, whose growls
are innocuous.   Still, in justice to Ouida, I
should deny that her hatred of women ever
reached anything like an offensive boiling-
point except in the early novel "Puck,"
which has probably done as much to feed
the spleen of her enemies as any work to

which she has given her name. In subsequent novels she has created many women of great sweetness and high-mindedness, as Etoile in "Friendship," Vera in "Moths," Wanda in the story of that title, Yseult in "Princess Napraxine," and Damaris in "Othmar." Perhaps a depraved and sinful woman is more execrable than a man of the same perverted traits. This is a question open to debate, though Ouida somehow suggests an opposite judgment. It is true that the majority of her very bad people are not men, though she is capable, at a pinch, of some darkly Mephistophelian types.

On the other hand, her love for the helpless and the unfriended, her profound charity toward the down-trodden and destitute and neglected among humanity, is one of the several bonds between her own genius and that of Hugo—a poet whom she resembles more than I have availed myself of opportunity to indicate.

But I do not claim that these words about Ouida—though I have called them "the truth," and though, as regards my own most sincere faith and equally sincere unfaith, I so insist upon calling them—are in any degree a satisfactory criticism. How

this woman's littleness dies into a shadow
beside her imaginative greatness, a real
critic will hereafter tell. I have already
stated in another essay my fixed belief
concerning the scientific method which
every critic who at all merits the place of
one should infallibly use. For myself, I
wish to be thought no more than that
purveyor of opinions whom I have previously sentenced with some emphasis. I
simply print what I think and believe about
Ouida, and I have declared it to be "the
truth" only as I see and realize truth. If
it be falsehood, I shall welcome with gladness any actual critic who so proves it.
But to satisfy me of my own errors he
must not by any means deport himself in
the same arbitrary and downright fashion
as I have done. He must bear in mind
that if he desires to convince me of my one-
sidedness he must not oppose it with *dicta*
as unfoundedly hypothetical as my own.
He must not be a man who profusely deals,
as I do, in unverified declarations. He
must logically elucidate to me where I am
wrong and why I am right. It occurs to
me, with that vanity of all essayists who
temporarily have the field quite to them-

selves, that I am more often right than wrong. But if I am conclusively proved more often wrong than right by that system of acute investigation which only the science-bred critic understands, then I shall still feel that I have been of marked service to the writer thus empirically reviewed ; for I shall at least have made myself a means of rousing careful and faithful consideration toward a series of imaginative works thus far either unreasonably contemned or irresponsibly lauded. The scientific tone and poise is so prevailing and favorite a one at the present time in works which a few years ago it rarely invaded, that I cannot help asking myself why the critics, who of all living persons are most easily accredited with the scientific tone and poise, should not more fondly and unhesitatingly employ it. They almost universally fail to employ it, however ; and on this account the wandering verbiage of their estimates may be said to be as valueless as the announcements which I now pluck up boldness enough to print. But my boldness has a weak fibre or two of cowardice in it, I fear, after all. I should never have presumed to write of Ouida as I

have written, had I not prized her compo-
sitions, frankly and *de bon cœur*, far more
than I blame them.   For this reason I have
given my favorable views publicity.   Ouida
is so internationally popular that I am
confident of friendly endorsements which
will mitigate for me the necessary agony
of being anathematized as her defender.
There my cowardice stops—in a certainty
of helpers and supporters.   For the rest,
if I am called names because I pay to a
reigning genius what I hold as her rightful
tribute, my stolid resignation will be equal
to any martyr's.   I shall endure the odium,
certain of its ultimate destruction.   Times
change, and I think the day is not far dis-
tant when Ouida will be amazed at the sov-
ereign fame which she herself has builded
through all these years of failure and tri-
umph, of weakness and power.   But perhaps she will not be astonished at all, being
dead.   Or perhaps . . .   But I leave that
point for the religionists and the agnostics
to fight out between themselves.   One gets
immortality of a certain kind, now and then,
whether *pallida mors* bring to us posthumous
beatitude, brimstone or annihilation.   And
Ouida, I should insist (with deference to the

coming scientific critic), has secured this terrene kind of immortality. I don't know whether or not she would rank it as a very precious boon. To judge from a good many passages in her abundant writing, I should be inclined to decide negatively.

SHOULD CRITICS BE GENTLEMEN?

Not long ago I received from a lady of
much culture and fine natural intelligence
a letter whose chief contents chanced to
bear upon a recent hostile newspaper notice of a book which she had herself cordially admired. One paragraph of this
letter especially struck me. It ran thus:

" The attack upon Mr. ——'s book has
served more than·ever to convince me that
there is something all wrong with modern
'criticism'—so called. Why should not
the same courtesy be preserved in writing
of a book which accepted usage forces
upon us in speaking of one before its author? Reckless personality is condemned
in social intercourse as vulgar, and even
odious; why should it be held admissible
the instant that the reviewer takes up his
pen? I remember hearing, as a school-girl,
of ' polite literature. Is politeness an im-
perative requisite of literature alone, or are
there similar kindly demands upon the

people who set themselves to consider it?
. .. . Suppose we put into actual life
the same ill-breeding which now exists
among the newspaper critics. My husband, as you know, is a Wall Street bank-
er. Imagine that some gentleman strolled
of a morning into his office, and instead of
the usual decent 'good-day,' began coolly
to assure him that his business ability was
overrated, that his financial success had
been cheaply purchased, that he owed his
present prosperity to a mere drift of luck,
and that, taken altogether, he was a person
of very little real consequence. I am
nearly certain that my husband, under such
circumstances, would become exceedingly
angry. And if he added to his anger a flat
request that this same outspoken individual should never again cross his threshold,
I am positive in my belief that hundreds
of thoughtful and fair-minded outsiders
would promptly support the course he had
taken. . . . The great difficulty with all
you literary people is that you almost
wholly waive good manners in your discussions of one another. You pour upon
the book of a fellow-writer abuse which
you would despise yourselves for venting
if it were a question of his ill-cut coat, his

inseparable squint or his hereditary freck-
les. You draw quite too sharp a line between what you may hold to be good criticism and what your own sense of common
propriety has long ago convinced you to
be good breeding."

This communication, after I had read
and pondered it, struck me as a somewhat
lucid view of the whole matter. If not a
comprehensive judgment, it is certainly
one which contains the true reformatory
element. There is perhaps no one of its
factors with which civilization could less
easily dispense than with that of courtesy.
Imagine the horrors of a drawing-room or
a dinner-table where everybody said to
everybody else precisely what he considered to be deserved or appropriate, regard-
less of the pain it would cost. In the republic of letters, it might be answered, we
are supposed to replace formality by sincerity. That is not unlike the method,
take it all in all, adopted by Robespierre
in *his* republic. There was a great deal of
sincerity about that. Critics and criticism
there had it all their own way. It was an
incisive way, and one essentially brutal.
For the latter reason its admirers were
numerous.

Censure would find it hard to adequately discountenance the arrogance and rude-
ness of the newspaper critic as they exist
at the present time. His effort to show
mental superiority and notable acumen
quite too often makes him forget that he
is also expected to appear a gentleman.
He may not be one (he is, alas! too frequently the dreary reverse), but he is nevertheless required to seem one by that very
standard of high cultivation which he has
so emphatically assumed. Even he would
admit that there is something in good
manners, after all. Only, it is difficult to
remember manners while you are being
radiantly judicial. The sun has beams
that kill. Is it so painful a calamity that
you should give some one poor Jones his
quietus while you illuminate your entire
period and pour consequent benefit on
many Joneses?

I know the modern critic to be a very
sensitive person,—quite as much so as the
most thin-skinned poet who ever bled under his bodkin. I have never been able
to explain this peculiarity except through
the tremulous effects of an evil conscience.
It is constantly manifest, however, and it
has more than once led me to realize the

keenness of those shocks which its possessor must find himself called on to sustain
when he encounters printed impressions of
fellow-critics diametrically different from
his own. That he is always finding himself disagreed with there can be no admissible doubt. I don't know what heroic
self-reliance buoys up his sense of infallibility under these trying conditions. For
my own part, I have more than once ex-
amined with amusement the variations between the verdicts passed by "authori-
ties" upon my own humble work. I have
read the eulogies of Rhadamanthus in the
Tomahawk till my cheeks tingled with
pleasurable blushes. " How entirely charming of Rhadamanthus !" I have said to
myself. "He understands me; he and I
are kindred souls, and the next time I
meet him on Broadway I hope it will be
lunch-time, so that I can ask him to join
me somewhere for a chop and a swallow
of claret." Then I have taken up the
Hatchet, and discovered that Minos thinks
I have just added new indignity to the
persecutions of an over-patient public. I
am styleless and flaccid; I am aspiring,
but effete; I have blundered into a pseudo-
reputation, and am a complex junction of

dulness, falsity and feebleness. This both alarms and depresses me. I ask myself, with the vague and meek ratiocination of one simultaneously petted and persecuted, how I can be, on account of the same piece of literary achievement, at once wise and foolish, profound and shallow, talented and vacuous. But the *Lancet* soon reassures me. I am, according to Æacos, neither large nor small; it is quite explained now: I am simply a nice blending of mediocrity and industry. Here are three mighty judges, all stoutly opposed to one another. They cannot all be right; and if one is right the other two are fatally wrong. But how shattering to my own impulses of reverence! It is like a vulgar family quarrel in the household of Jupiter.

These discordances of opinion are not occasional; they occur every day. They are to my mind the great proof of how absurdly needless are all published comments on books in current newspapers. Many an author might find two or three of his works adorning the "parlor table" of some "flat" in Harlem owned by the reviewer who has hotly abused them all during past months. This gentleman has no doubt

forgotten his own abuse. Perhaps he has
really read the books afterward, unpro-
fessionally, as it were, in the quiet of his
own home and beneath the light of his
evening lamp, enjoying their contents.
Most fair and thoughtful criticism is of
necessity kindly, and you are very apt to
cut a sorry figure in recommending a book
which you have not thoroughly read. In
nine cases out of ten your praise rings false
and silly, for your ignorance of what you
are praising betrays itself, like the piece
of futile hypocrisy it is. You resemble a
maid who rouges her mistress in a dim
light; there is danger of the lady's nose
getting a little rosy accidental spot on its
tip. But the criticism that puts down its
head like a bull and " makes " for a book
never requires the least preparation, pre-
meditation. Not very long ago I met a
critic who engaged me in conversation on
the subject of more than one recent book
which I myself happened carefully to have
read, and which he had presumably read,
as he had reviewed each of them. To my
surprise, he spoke of one these books in
tones of extreme praise. He had forgotten, no doubt, that he had ever denounced
it. I could not help feeling that I should

altogether have preferred this gentleman's blame.

Nothing is so easy as to be what we nowadays call a critic. Unless you are mentally unsound, you must have certain opinions regarding the books which may come under your eye. Entertaining such opinions, you are required to express them with moderate ease and glibness, though the integrity demanded of your syntax will, I suppose, vary according to the "tone" of your journal or the liberality of your wage. For my own part, when reflecting that I too possess, in common with the rest of my race, opinions about the literary performances of my contemporaries, I cannot but feel that I would sell almost anything else in the world rather than become a daily—or weekly—vender of these opinions. Oranges, bananas, gentlemen's braces, lead-pencils—you may go through a very long list of salable things (if you will only leave me my good name), and I feel certain that you will hit upon nothing which I should not prefer to sell rather than these inevitably haphazard and often grossly unjust personal opinions. I have not the slightest doubt that some future day will see newspaper criticism as completely abolished as the whipping-post, the stocks, imprisonment for debt and other exploded nuisances.

The first delicious sense of power in a young writer is always accompanied by a conviction that he can teach others how to write and how not to write. He may himself have done nothing more noteworthy than a few lyrics in the *Waverley Magazine*, that publication which takes pride, I am informed, in asserting that it thrives upon the *cacoëthes* of the would-be Tennysons and Thackerays, and which boasts of never having paid a dollar for any of the extraordinary verses and stories thronging its innumerable pages. He may only have written a vapid little tale for some local journal,—let us say in Brundusium, Ohio, —or a peppery editorial or two in the pages of a sheet eagerly subscribed for by the citizens of Gomorrah, Wyoming Territory. But he will feel himself a critic, just the same. Give him his head, and he will scamper rough-shod over Dante and Robert Louis Stevenson, Milton and Henry James, with the same unsparing ardor of treatment. He will adore, he will hate ; he will dissect, he will generalize ; he will vituperate, he will condone ; he will scorn, he will wor-

ship. In other words, he possesses prejudices *pro* and *con*, for which he desires un-
restricted vent. If the editor of the New
York *Tribune* were to advertise for a critic
to-morrow, I have no doubt that the appli-
cants for such office would swiftly swell
into thousands throughout a single day.
The one thing that all literary tyros believe
themselves capable of doing, and of doing
superlatively well, is criticism upon writers
of recognized name. They think it, in the
words of the old phrase, to be "as easy as
lying;" and I regret to add that in other
respects they often make it not dissimilar
from that wide-spread weakness. Newspaper offices naturally swarm with persons
of just this analytic and ambitious turn.
The editors will tell you that many more
neophytes aspire to do "review work" than
to embark upon the mundane reportorial
drudgeries. It is chiefly from these very
self-sufficient and audacious beings that the
author receives his worst assaults. The
world appears to perceive that this is true,
and yet with regard to the author himself
it rather curiously misunderstands and mis-
values the whole situation. "Do not notice
your critics!" it cries to the indignant victim, about whose ears peas from ambus-

caded shooters may be whizzing, and with
some annoyance if with no actual peril.
"They are quite beneath you. It is in the
worst possible taste for you to show the
least consciousness on your part that they
exist at all." But meanwhile the injured
author, recipient as he so often is of absolute insult, finds himself called upon to observe that the world gives his critics a fair
share of respectful attention. My own ex-
periences of this self-contradictory movement have been rather amusing. I have
on certain occasions inly smiled as I heard
comments delivered to me upon my own
works which echoed with a servility that
was perhaps unconscious more than a single
statement extant in yesterday's newspaper.
Whether, indeed, the general reading public does concern itself with these observa-
tions is, after all, questionable ; but it is
true that there are two classes who do
peruse them and often study them carefully
as well—an author's friends and his enemies. This is a constituency which never
fails the most spiteful reviewer, and it is
one upon which he counts in the main-
tenance of his wholly useless position.

I insist that it is in every case a useless
position, even when it is charitably rather

than maliciously maintained. Newspaper
critics are as little wanted as newspaper
advertisements are greatly wanted—and
paid for on that account. Publishers send
books to the daily or weekly press with but
one motive—that they shall be copiously
praised. Some three or four volumes of a
work are for this reason given away whenever publication occurs. The distribution
is made for commercial reasons alone, and
the publishers, through slender sales, are
often losers because of it. Upon them the
loss alone falls ; they are so many copies
"out." They read adverse notices—too frequently tissues of reckless falsehood when
not the product of minds either jaded from
underpaid overwork or by nature meagrely
equipped for the tasks entered upon—with
a bitterness quite as acute as the author's.
Hostility that touches a man's pocket irri-
tates him quite as much as that which
touches his self-esteem. Publishers are to-
day groaning at the churlish paragraphic
treatment which their gratuitous copies
receive from newspapers to which they are
sent. And yet these gentlemen still continue to send. They recognize the absurdity,
the foolhardiness, of the whole system, but,
like many another abuse, it obtains because

it has become time-honored, and they still
go on practically sanctioning it.   A few
months ago I received from a publisher of
excellent standing and universally accepted
shrewdness a declaration that surprised me
because of its unexpected frankness.   It
was distinctly to the effect that he himself
would be glad enough to do away with the
whole custom of offering books for journal-
istic attention and discussion, provided
three or four houses of similar repute to
his own would agree upon a similar course.
But there lay the fatal impediment.   His
confrères were always hoping that a book
issued by them would have the luck to
secure wide approval from the critics, be
written about in one homogeneous strain
of praise from Vermont to Utah, and hence
secure a "boom" that would swell financial
receipts afterward.   But such a golden
trouvaille of good fortune is very rarely hit
upon.   It is nearly always the same order
of things with the despots of the many
petty provinces.   They may be clad with a
little brief authority, but they propose to
get all the wear procurable out of this
flimsy and transient vestment.   They are
determined to strut about in it, to drape its
folds, as might be said, with a becoming

personal dignity. Tompkins would not
write of the last novel or poem or biogra-
phy as Smith has done for even an extra
dollar a week added to his pathetic salary ;
and there are nine chances out of ten that
Brown will feel himself equally thrilled by
his own individualism and mental importance when examining the decisions of
Tompkins or Smith. No ; the commercial
value of the whole arbitrary and whimsical
process is almost always *nil* to the aggrieved
publisher. He finds that as a rule his
"selling" books are those which the critics
treat even more shabbily than usual, or
concerning which they disagree with an
unwonted ardor. He feels in his heart that
the newspaper is to be trusted simply as a
medium of information between himself
and his public, declaring that certain works
have been issued by him, and can be bought
just as he has bought the means of so
asserting. He has a full perception of the
flippancy, the acrimony and the incom-
petence by which his donations are inces-
santly rewarded. And he still makes them,
notwithstanding. Some day there will be
a quiet and effectual revolt against this
flagrant injustice. Some day the wrong
will right itself, and instead of receiving

bundles of new books by the morning mail or express, that sapient institution, our modern newspaper, will find the avowal of its literary loves and hates alike unsolicited. Such a prophecy may sound millennial; so does that of an international copyright law, whose absence makes us properly the jeer of almost every other civilized nation, and turns all our authors into men without countries. But one day we shall have international copyright, nevertheless, just as one day we shall carelessly and almost unconsciously dispense with all such minor tyrannies as newspaper critics.

As an example of extreme sincerity and honesty among members of this guild, I should like to chronicle a particular incident which befell myself. One evening, about eight years ago, just before the appearance of my first book of poems, "Fantasy and Passion," I went to a reception given at the Lotos Club, in New York. Among the assembled guests was a certain person whom some optimists have seriously stated to be a poet. He had a position, then, upon some evening paper as its literary critic; I am not quite sure whether or no it was the journal which he at present represents, though I think not. He had

been writing with belligerence and not a
little clear malignity about certain poems
of mine in the *Atlantic Monthly* and elsewhere, and when I received from a mutual
acquaintance his request to cross the rooms
and speak with him, I felt considerable
surprise. After very little hesitation, however, I refused point-blank; and yet I sent
no uncivil message, since the whole affair
was one of quite too much indifference to
me for that. As I subsequently learned,
however, he became excessively angry on
hearing of my unwillingness, and indeed
lost all control of his temper. "I will kill
that man!" he exclaimed to my peaceful
and astonished emissary, finishing his sentence with a robust oath, and beginning
his next sentence with another. "By ——,
I've killed bigger men than he is, and I'll
kill *him!*" This murderous threat bore no
allusion to my own life, but rather to that
of my first book of poems, "Fantasy and
Passion." On the appearance of that book,
the gentleman certainly behaved like a
critic with a private graveyard for the
corpses of those reputations which he had
already wrathfully slain. Whether he succeeded in burying my own there or not I
leave his most amiable conscience to decide.

I seem to have somehow risen from my ashes, if this is true ; but it may be only one of those delusions born of an author's inextinguishable egotism, even after he himself has been given a permanent quietus.

But I deny that the least egotism has impelled me to record this dramatic little episode. I have merely wished to show what exquisite fidelity to principles, what honorable discharge of responsibility, may exist among these critics of newspapers, from whom we are entitled surely to expect an unbiassed and disinterested expression of their likes and dislikes, if nothing more final and valuable. There is no part of my narration at all doubtful as to fact. The gentleman who was a witness of this critic's fine rageful outburst and an auditor of his anathema, made no mistake in what he saw and heard. Now, let us consider, from an article signed with his own name in a recent issue of his journal, just what philosophic and flawless theories of criticism this reviewer, who vowed he would kill me and who has killed bigger men than I am, fosters enough diverting effrontery to print. "They," writes our Thalaba, alluding to certain other reviewers whom his own rancorous postulates have offended, "might keep their temper, as I do mine, and *they need not attribute personal motives to me, for I have none. No man who is worthy of the name of a critic ever writes from a personal motive.* His business is not to deal with the author, the artist, the actor, but with his work." Yes, my lusty arch-foe, you are for once wholly right. And you might have added, "His business is also not to growl profane and ridiculous menaces against an author whose book he has not yet even seen, and then to indulge in slanderous comments regarding that author, whenever occasion serves, during a period of eight succeeding years." I can scarcely explain why memory wanders just here to that tragic incident in "Pendennis" where the "Spring Annual" containing poor Pen's verses (and very lovely verses they were, as we all recall in thinking of "The Church Porch") fell into the hands of Mr. Bludyer. "Mr. Bludyer," runs the passage, "who was a man of very considerable talent, . . . had a certain notoriety in his profession, and reputation for savage humor. He smashed and trampled down the poor spring-flowers with no more mercy than a bull would have on a parterre; and, having cut up the volume to his heart's content, went and sold it at a book-stall, and purchased a pint of brandy with the proceeds of the volume."

I am well aware that it is nowadays the fashion for authors not to "answer" their critics. If Byron should write his " English Bards and Scotch Reviewers" at the present time, its pungent satire would be denounced as in execrable taste, and all his friends would pull long faces when they met him, in sorrow at his exceeding temerity. The newspapers are now supposed to be omnipotent in crushing a man, and to " fight" them, as the phrase goes, is looked upon as courting sure destruction. But while the law mercifully draws a line at positive libel, I cannot see just why the publicity which they are capable of causing should deter an honest man or an honest woman from resenting outrage. If you are reviled because you have dared to write a book, I fail to understand why you should shrink from a little more abuse for denying false charges against it. You say to me, my friend, that I should hold all critics in contempt. So I will, when the publishers refrain from holding them in respect. So I will, when I cease to find their praise used in advertisements of my

works, like the certificate of a schoolboy's
good conduct. So I will, when I know
them receiving disregard, and not propitia-
tion. So I will, when society says to me,
" It is a very serious and great art, this art
of criticism, and it is neither the ruffianly
swinging of a bludgeon nor the insecure
handling of a scalpel."

It seems to me that if a true critic should
arise in the world he would be as worthy
of homage and reverence as the noblest
philosopher or poet who ever lived. He
would be as dispassionate as the law of
gravitation and as charitable as the all-
dispensing sun. But, alas! when and
where have we had a true critic ? Emerson ? He is as divine in his misjudgments
as he is trustworthy in his splendid intui-
tions. Carlyle ? He was a *poseur*, a shrieker,
who scolded ostentatiously and made people remark his tempest because it was en-
closed in so fantastic a teapot. Besides,
these men were not literary critics in any
true sense. But Taine, the remarkable and
brilliant Taine, is a literary critic ; and yet
who can forgive him for being so much of a
Frenchman as to put De Musset above Tennyson ? There is no criticism at all except
that which founds itself upon inflexible,

logical science. If beauty, eloquence, poetry, rhythm, harmony, style, taste, insight
into human character, sympathy with the
phases and subtleties of nature, are not
susceptible of scientific definition and clas-
sification, they are not truth—for all truth
is so susceptible, sooner or later. It will
not do for A to tell me that Poe's "Annabel Lee" has an "indefinable melody,"
an "unfathomable tenderness." B, who
does not see with the eyes of A at all, may
think "Annabel Lee" a mere sensuous and
senseless jingle. Both sides may rave, for
and against, over the merits or the short-
comings of these stanzas. But enthusiasm settles no more than vituperation does.
De gustibus non disputandum is a sword of
epigram that simply tries to cut the throat
of criticism. I do not mean that he who
tells me why a poem is beautiful should
explain to me what beauty *is*. He can no
more do that than he can tell me what
matter is when he states that one mass of
it, the earth, moves round another mass of
it, the sun. But he can find some living
law — as I almost believe the German
thinker, Schopenhauer, has done—which
governs beauty in all its forms of development and manifestation. All modern crit-

icism is summed up in this: "I, John
Smith, declare that John Brown has or has
not genius, has or has not ability, is or is
not a poet, a philosopher, a historian, a
novelist." We are overrun with essays and
disquisitions on writers ; we are surfeited
with *ipse dixi ;* we have had enough and
more than enough of *a priori* dogmatism.
I know that there are a great many people
who are prepared to shudder at the thought
of science being applied to any of their
æsthetic pleasures. Whenever it is a question of their-bodily health, of the bread they
eat, of the air they breathe, of the clothes
they wear, of the colds they catch, of the
deaths they are likely to die, they accept the
only aid and guidance which their reason
assures them to be the potent one. But
with literature they must indulge a sentimental acceptance of the inscrutable. It
appears to me that newspaper critics and
all the numberless foibles which their random *dicta* beget are a result of just this
drowsy bigotry. "How," cries the quiver-
ing voice of sentimentality, "can you demonstrate to me the fragrance of the rose
or the whiteness of the lily?" My answer
must be, "I can do neither ultimately, but
I can do both relatively. If I were a news-

paper critic, I might assert that the rose was odorless and the lily blood-red. These would be statements quite as unsupported by proof as many which stare at us from the pages of our morning journals, in their 'literary' columns. But I can prove inductively and comparatively, if you will, that *to you* the odor diffused by your rose has a right to be called agreeable, and similarly that the purity of your lily has a right to be called chaste." I am prone to believe that very marvellous things may be done in literature when this abhorred science has begun to investigate it. There must be very powerful radical reasons why we are all so willing to think "Hamlet" a work of genius. Thus far nearly all the writers who have told us why have considered rather too much who is telling it and how it is being told. The paths of the essayist and the analyst are widely divergent. One is full of the pretty buds of rhetoric—the *flosculi sententiarum*—which it is hard not occasionally to stop and pluck. The other is bloomless, and even granitic, with no temptations for the rhapsodist over floriculture, and a very stern method in the recurrence of its mile-stones.

There is a publishing-house in New York

—that of Messrs. Funk & Wagnalls, if I may
be permitted to mention its name without
bringing on myself the awful accusation of
wishing to " puff " it—which has struck me
as having hit, in the turmoil and fatuity of
newspaper criticism, upon a mode of win-
ning public attention at once legitimate
and salutary. This house has conceived
the plan of sending to authors of established fame copies of the new books which
it has issued, and asking from them a few
lines, to be printed as advertisement if
thought advisable. Surely this attitude, if
persistently perserved, is one which in time
could be made stoutly to prevail over all
the haphazard treatises of the ordinary reviewers. If the author under consideration, whoever he may be, could look into
the columns of a newspaper and find that
Tennyson, Mr. Herbert Spencer, Mr. Lecky,
Mr. Tyndall or Mr. Froude had not only
praised his work, but allowed such praise
to be openly published as a help to him
against the puerilities and jealousies of the
mere empirical bunglers, how thankful he
might have good reason to feel ! And
even if lesser writers could be brought to
lend each other their warm, sweet aid,
whenever they could truthfully and sin-

cerely do so, what a gentle but telling fight
would be waged against those wrangling
" professionals" who now swarm about a
book like minnows round a freshly-dropped
bait ! True enough, there would be no
real criticism in all this. It would be a
compromise, not a settlement ; an improvement, not a remedy. Authors are not critics, because all individual talent (or genius,
which is precisely the same as talent in
kind, though not in degree) presupposes
limitation. But authors are in most cases
vastly better critics than the so-termed
critics themselves. I know with what de-
rision the latter might feel inclined to hail
my statement. It would be as extraordinary, if they did not so hail it, as the
popularization of agnosticism among the
clergy. And yet if you, reader, had written
a poem, whom would you choose to have
for its eulogist ? The Dryasdust who glares
at it with a preconceived hatred because
the Muses are nine and so are the children
whom he has to support by hack-work on
the *Saturday Scorpion ?* Or would your pref-
erence be just one brief sentence from the
wise and tender lips of such a man as the
late Mr. Longfellow? Whose approval
would please you more ? Would not the

first, indeed, turn to utter tameness beside
the last? Surely yes, I think, although
few poets have ever been more infamously
assailed in their time than Longfellow was.
I remember that once while I·was a guest
in his lovely home our conversation drifted
upon critics. His mild, lucid eye almost
flashed as he said to me, "Whenever I have
been attacked by one of those fellows I
always feel as if I had been blackguarded
in the street!" This may prove interesting to a few of "those fellows" who still
live ; but, whether it does or not, I repeat
Longfellow's exact words. A little later,
during that same visit, he said to me,
"Never notice your critics, under any circumstances." And I have always remembered the little gesture of disdain that went
with these words ; for Longfellow was by
no means the milk-and-water personage
whom some of his biographers have painted
him, but a man of the world, trained in the
choicest niceties and elegances, and with a
savoir-faire and dignity of demeanor that
I have seldom seen equalled. Even if he
had not been the true and noble poet he
was, he could never have become a critic ;
his manners were far too good for that.
In allusion to Poe's pitiable dirt-throwing,

he spoke with the gentlest reserve ; and yet
he told me, shaking his head for a moment
with evident melancholy, that Poe was in
his debt for a considerable sum of money
at the period this scurrilous onslaught had
been made. Well, time has been the
avenger, and Poe's meanness has borne no
fruit. The fame of Longfellow will stay
luminous for generations to be, while that
of Poe, in the poetical sense, is kept fever-
ishly alive by fanatical admirers whom the
meretricious tawdriness of his verse (apart
from the really astonishing quality of his
prose) fails to convince that he was by no
means a poet. I have always been able to
understand just why Poe was so ferocious,
narrow and ungentlemanly a "critic" of
other men's writing since I heard the words
of a man who had once seen and talked
with him. The man was a printer, the
head of a reputable printing establishment,
and what he communicated to me regarding his single experience of Poe I then had
every reason to believe, and still believe
implicitly. "I once saw Edgar Poe," declared my informant, "and shall never
forget the meeting. He called upon me
and made to me a proposition regarding a
newspaper which he wished to establish.

IIis proposition was thoroughly immoral, involving a distinct scheme of fraud, and his condition when he made it was one of the most revolting drunkenness." If Poe had ever succeeded in starting that newspaper, we can easily imagine, from the insolent personalities which some of his miscellanies now contain, how detestable would have been its "critical" posture. What he wrote in it regarding his contemporaries would probably have been as foolish as his poetry, and a great deal more poisonous. As a weaver of wondrous romances his exceptional intellect deserves all honor ; but when he attitudinizes as a newspaper critic he almost teaches us to forget "The Fall of the House of Usher" and "The Cask of Amontillado," while we remember vividly enough the strut and nonsense of "Ulalume" and the verbose, theatrical prolixity of "The Raven." Scientific criticism can make plain enough just why such poems as these are worthless, and a like test will serve, I am very certain, to demolish as equally trivial the volleys poured upon Longfellow and others.

If all the misery, the despondency, the feeling of brutal wrong and the despairing apathy which has resulted from newspaper criticism could be massed together in one dolorous chapter, such accumulation would form a tragedy horrible past thought. No writer has ever been young and striven who has not passed through stages of needless pain at comments which are sometimes bruited abroad concerning his work by people who might not wish, in the ordinary following of their lives, to injure a fly. Gifford may not have really killed Keats, after all : I hope there never has been a Gifford in the world strong enough to kill, or a Keats weak enough to let him self be killed.   But if the free lances of the press really could see the red and vital blood which their calumnious thrusts will sometimes draw from young and sensitive breasts, I am confident that they would blush with shame as red as the blood itself. I have thought a great deal on the subject, and I am wholly unable to understand why a young man who publishes a trashy novel, or a trashy poem, or a trashy anything else, should have it fulminated against in the newspapers.   It may be as bad as human intelligence can conceive of, and it may write its author down an ass fifty times over. But it is nearly always a work of perfectly unconscious absurdity. I have always suspected that the "Sweet Singer of Michigan" was a clever man or woman who played a deliberate part in those apparently well-intentioned stanzas of his or hers. But there are many singers who believe themselves to be sweet and are not, and who have got into print, and yet who possess nerve-centres, capacities for trembling under fierce rebuff, organizations fit to thrill with quite as much emotion as their verses are powerless to express. Why rail against these harmless victims of an illusive will-o'-the-wisp? Why call them names, and stamp upon them, and question Jove himself as to the object of their creation? No service to literature is done by giving them sleepless nights and days of torment. Their feeble books are perfectly sure of dying, without denunciation being hurled at them the moment they are born. Nobody will read them, in any case. Pray do not flatter yourself, fiery-eyed critic, with your furious foot still upon one of their gilt-edged offspring, that you have performed the slightest public benefit by your frenzy of condemnation. You have

simply succeeded in making a fellow-crea-
ture's heart suffer—nothing more. Your
rodomontade was not at all wanted ; society could have done quite as well without
it. The world at large has the same reluctance to buy the book of a new author
that you or I may have to strike an
acquaintance with some plausible person
who accosts us on a steamboat or a railway-
car. And with the author of fixed position
it is very much the same. He has won his
spurs, and you critics can neither burnish
them brighter nor cast upon them the least
film of tarnish. There is more potency in
a word or two, favorable or unfavorable,
about my last book, delivered by X—— to
Z—— over their friendly dinner, than in all
the glory of your panegyric or all the darkness of your diatribe. Leave the authors
alone, and their destinies are just as certain
as though you did not seek to manipulate
them. A good book was never yet made
unpopular because you contemned it, nor
a poor one salable because you shouted in
its behalf. The community can find out
what they want to read without your multiplex and bewildering counsel. There is
one thing that you can do, and I am im-

pressed with an idea that you do it most
pertinaciously and relentlessly : you can
inflict torture upon the callow authors and
sharp annoyance upon the veteran ones.
Don't believe any author, though his hair
be as white as eighty years can turn it,
when he tells you that he doesn't care for
your stabs and pin-pricks. Of course he
cares. I will warrant you he is a pretty
tepid and spineless kind of an author if he
does not. Would not you care, messieurs,
if you were trying to ford a muddy street,
and a troop of vicious roysterers passed
you in another direction, splashing the mud
farther than your boots—as far even as
your eyes ? Mud is mud, you know, gentlemen, no matter who throws it at one.
It dries easily, and Jane the housemaid or
John the valet can quite nicely dust it
from one's trousars or waistcoat the next
morning. But you have a disagreeable
after-thought, nevertheless, of how easy it
would have been for those riotous persons
who met you yesterday not to have cast
it.

I should like for once to see and shake
hands with a newspaper critic who had no
conscientious belief that he was one of the

guardians at the gates of his national literature. It would be delightful to find so welcome a product of modern intelligence. I should naturally object to him for being a newspaper critic at all, but I should control that objection without difficulty because of gratitude at his charming rarity. If it were in my power to secure him a clerkship in a bank, a position in the custom-house, how gladly I would offer to do so! And I am certain he would accept with alacrity, for he would be so anxious to leave the company of his fellow-critics, who all had convinced themselves that they held, each one, an especial grip upon the wheel that moves public appreciation this way or that. Ah, let such autocrats as these go to their elders, who have passed years in supposably moulding the fates of authors. Let them ask such warriors in a trifling war if they honestly think they have ever either slain or saved an author. I fancy that I know what the answer will be, if it is truly an honest one. And then comes the irreversible question: Why harass and retard and irritate energies which, after all, provided they be energies of the slightest real momentum, must finally brush away such embarrassments as if they were gnats? Learn your trade, gentlemen (or your art, if it be an art), before you attempt to practise it. Science points you the path, not whim or conceit or vainglory. It is a straight path, but a clear one. And its first foothold, if I mistake not, is humane courtesy.